Rocksta Daddy

written by
K.T. Fisher

Rockstar Daddy
(Book 1 in the Decoy Series)

Copyright @2013 Kellie Fisher
Cover art @2013 CT COVER CREATIONS

This is a work of fiction. Names, characters, places and incidents are either the product of the author's imagination or are used fictitiously. Any resemblance to any actual persons living or dead, businesses and events or locales are entirely coincidental.

Prologue

Kendal

"Is it time?"

I look to my best friend Jessica, who's sitting on the edge of my bed. She checks her phone and nods her head slowly. I walk towards my little bathroom where I left the pregnancy test sitting on the edge of the bath. I couldn't sit in the same room with it. It felt like it was screaming at me and demanding attention. I feel sick to my stomach I'm that nervous. I can't believe I am having to do this! I'm twenty years old, I'm too young to be a mum. On the plus side, I knew who the father of my baby. I suppose that's good news. It doesn't make me feel any better though.

I have been with my boyfriend, Jax for two years. He is amazing. He's six feet tall, has big, broad shoulders, messy jet black hair, and smoky gray eyes that could heat my body with a certain look. He screams sex appeal with that sexy V right below his toned and well-muscled stomach. I get horny just looking at him. That's probably why I'm in this mess to begin with - because we have so much fun enjoying each other's bodies. No matter how often we did it, we could not seem to satisfy that need for each other. The only problem is that other girls also get flushed when they are around Jax. They throw themselves at him even when we're together, which pisses me off but it's all part of the deal because he's the lead singer of a rock band called Decoy.

The band is becoming really popular, and that means more attention from the girls. When he's on that stage, they all scream for him. He assures me that he loves me and he doesn't want any other girl. I believe and trust him with all my heart, but this is just the beginning. Since the band is composed of four good-looking men, they have a lot of groupies. His band mates Rhys, Leo, and Max take advantage of all the beautiful girls who follow them around. I feel like I'm keeping Jax back. It's not that I hate what Jax does. I just did't want to keep him from living his dreams, and having a girlfriend while being on the fast track to becoming a famous rock star can keep you from a lot of things. I love him so much and I feel like I'm keeping him back. Crazy, right? What kind of girl wants to dump her sexy rocker boyfriend, so that he can tour with his band and enjoy the rocker lifestyle and the girls that come with it? Oh yeah. That's me.

My friends Sam, Mark, and James act like my big overprotective brothers. The fact that my boyfriend is in a rock band doesn't go over well with them. Sam is the most pissed of the three because I take his girlfriend, and my best friend Jessica to Decoy's gigs with me. I assure them that we are perfectly safe because the guys in the band look after us. I think that is one of the reasons why Sam does not like Jessica being there. All the guys in the band are seriously good looking. Obviously, I think Jax is the hottest but the other guys get just as much attention. Max, Leo, and Rhys can be very flirtatious. They keep it to a minimum with me because I'm Jax's girl, but since they're not truly friends with Sam, they don't hold back where Jessica is concerned. Lately, I've started to bring along Tanya, a girl I met at college. She's pretty cool and loves their music, plus she's single so there's no jealous boyfriend on my case.

I reach for the pregnancy test and take a quick glance. My heart sinks and my whole world stops. Two lines, that means it's positive! Shit, I cannot be pregnant. I was sure we were safe all the time. I mean, I forgot my pill a couple of times but then I made sure Jax wrapped up or did the naughty pull out trick. I suppose that was dumb of us and did not actually work, because why else would I be standing here staring at two lines?

I walk out of the bathroom and as soon as I lock eyes with my best friend of ten years, I break down. She comes running over to me and I cry in her arms for what feels like hours. She smooths my bright red hair out of my face and looks me right in the eyes.

"What are you gonna do Kendal?"

I know I cannot have an abortion. That is just not me, I could never do that. My parents are going to kill me! Oh no, I'm going to trap Jax. I still have to finish college.

"I'm keeping the baby, but I don't know what I'm going to do about Jax."

Jess scrunches up her nose in confusion.

"Jax? What do you mean? He's the baby's dad."

"I cannot do this to him, Jess. He has his band to think about. I've nearly finished college, so I can get a job. I can support the baby on my own."

"Kendal, you cannot do that. He has to know you're pregnant. It is his baby too, so it's his responsibility as well. He will help you through all of this. It is not just your fault, you both did this. Let him help you."

I shake my head no. I know he will stand by me, which is why I cannot tell him. He will hate me for taking away his dream. I do not want to trap him and make him get a job he hates just to provide for me and our baby. I can do this, Jax does not need to know.

"I can do it on my own. I will get my own place so I'm not under my parents' feet. I can't do this to him, Jess. I love him too much. I cannot take away his dream."

Jessica lowers her head and sighs deeply.

"I think it is a very bad idea but it's not my choice to make. I will stand by you whatever you decide."

We hug and I cry some more. I have to end this with Jax tonight before I change my mind. Funny how just moments ago, I felt like my world was falling apart. Now I know exactly what I'm going to do.

Chapter 1

Kendal

Four years later

"OK, I think you've looked at that long enough."

Jessica snatches the newspaper away that I was helplessly staring at. There's a big picture of Decoy inside, listing everything they won last night at the music awards. Typically, none of them are wearing suits. Jessica shoves the newspaper into her huge handbag so it's out of my sight. I feel a stabbing pain in my heart from looking at the picture, Jax is still unbelievably gorgeous. I've never managed to get over him, I guess it's payback for leaving him without telling him I was pregnant with his baby. What's even worse is that I know I'll never be able to move on.

"Have you heard from Harley?"

Jessica takes the seat opposite me and places her cup of tea on the kitchen table.

"He text me yesterday to ask how Finley and I are doing."

Harley became my ex boyfriend three months ago. He's a great guy and absolutely gorgeous, he loved Finley and Finley seemed to really like him back. Unfortunately, I didn't return the same feelings Harley held for me. He gave me a shock when he asked me to move in with him. We were seeing each other for almost a year and I didn't realize he was heading in that direction, I thought we were having fun. I did't want anything serious. I couldn't move on from Jax to Harley because my heart still wants Jax. I had no choice but to end it with Harley.

"I'm back mummmmy!"

There goes my peace and quiet. At least Jessica can stop talking about my love life now. I look towards the kitchen doorway, and my heart skips a beat. Finley is standing there in black skinny jeans and a red t-shirt. How am I supposed to forget about Jax when I have his mini version living with me?

Finley jumps up onto my knees and wraps his little arms around my neck. God, I love this kid, I just can't but help feel guilty that Jax is missing out.

Jax

As soon as I wake up, I feel a hangover creeping over me. After we won four awards, we did what rock bands do best. There are certain parts of last night where my memories are fuzzy. God only knows how I managed to make it back to my hotel room.

The bed shifts beside me and I stop rubbing my hands over my face. I peek through my fingers, I see blonde hair sprawled out on the pillow next to mine. I hold back a groan of frustration.

Fuck!

So I guess I spent another night having drunk and meaningless sex. Yet another one night stand. It may be hard to believe, but I don't want this anymore, girl after girl with no strings or any kind future. It's not me anymore, it's boring.

I'd love for the blonde hair to turn bright red and the random girl would be replaced with the girl I miss so much. A girl who left me four years ago, Kendal Moore. Even her name makes my dick twitch. She was so sexy with a body that had the most delicious curves I've ever seen. Kendal had beautiful big blue eyes and creamy skin that was so smooth. I had the most amazing sex with her. We would have each other anywhere and any time we wanted. We were crazy about each other, and with Kendal sex was never meaningless. Each time was better than the last.

Here I am four years later, she's not even here and my dick is rock hard at just the thought of her. Kendal is the girl that got away, actually, she sort of ran away.

Over the years I've tried to fill Kendal's absence with one night stands.

A lot of them, don't get me wrong the girls were all gorgeous. I had my pick of groupies, models, and celebrities. None of them made me forget, none of them even came close to Kendal. I loved her and I think I still do, I've never been able to move on. She never looked at me like the girls do now. All other women look at me as Jax, the front man of Decoy. But Kendal wouldn't be bothered about all that. She was interested in me, she just wanted Jax Finley Parker. That was what I thought anyway because I thought she loved me.

When one night stands didn't work, I tried a relationship. That was a fucking huge mistake I wish I never made. Her name was Cheryl Daniels. She's a stunning woman with long black hair, slim body, chocolate brown eyes and huge fake tits. No matter how many times we had sex and spent time together, I didn't develop feelings for her. As soon as she told me she loved me, I had to call quits. I still see Cheryl from time to time, seeing as we're both in the public eye and she makes it obvious that she wants me back. I'm not interested at all because now that I'm not with her, I can see right through her. She was using me to boost her career right from the start. She just wanted me for publicity reasons.

The blonde beside me starts to wake up. As soon as her eyes open, she flashes me a seductive smile. I grimace at the sight, she looks rough as hell. Her hair is a mess and her make up is smudged all over her face.

"Hey sexy."

She purrs and rolls onto her side, revealing her large tits. I nod, I really don't want to talk right now. I'm pissed at myself, this shit has to stop. Blondie reaches out her hand and places it on top of my bare chest.

"You wanna go again? We could spend the day together. I'll let you do anything you like."

I bet she would but I need a hot shower to get the smell of sex and alcohol off me. I need to act like a dick so she will leave.

"I have shit to do. Why don't you grab your stuff and head out, yeah?"

She pouts her lips and scoots a little closer to me. The hand that was on my chest is slowly making its way down south and takes hold of my dick.

"Someone's happy to see me."

No darling it's a mixture of thinking about my ex and a morning glory. In a blur, she has her mouth around my cock, she's groans out loud against my dick but I don't even feel anything. She's bouncing her head up and down making all sorts of noises, I grab hold of her head to pull her off.

"I have shit to do babe. Another time, yeah?"

She whines and does that annoying pout again.

"Let's have some fun first."

"Look, I need you to go so I can take a shower."

I reach for my phone on the bedside table and jump out of bed. I know as I walk to the bathroom that I'm giving blondie a good view of my arse, but I don't give a shit. Before I close the door, I hear her shout behind me.

"I could join you in there?"

Does she not understand rejection?

"That's unnecessary."

As soon as the door shuts behind me, I look through the list of names in my phone until I find Steve. He's one of the few roadies that came back to London with us, he's used to getting rid of groupies who want to stick around. We decided that now the tour was finished, we would take a much needed break. In a few months, we are planning on writing our new album so we all decided to come back home and settle down here. We all missed our home town. Rhys and I are sick of not having a permanent home.

Steve tells me he will be here in five minutes. I pop my head out the door and see the blonde is now sitting up in the middle of the bed wearing her underwear. There's a handbag open and make up is scattered on the bed. She is holding a mirror up to her face and wiping away the make up from the previous night. It's a telltale sign that she's a groupie. She lifts her head up when she hears me open the door and smiles at me. She's probably thinking I've changed my mind about the shower.

"Someone will be here to take you home."

Her smile drops but I don't give a shit. I shut the door and lock it to be safe from the girl, I jump into the shower and take my time. Hopefully she'll be gone when I'm done.

Wrapping a towel around my bottom half when I get out, I look at my phone and see I have a message.

RHYS: Hey man. Did u manage 2 shake the blonde? The Mrs wants 2 have u all round 4 a big roast dinner. U know our room right? B here in an hour.

A big roast dinner is exactly what I need right now. Delicious home made meals are a rare thing when you're on the road touring.

ME: Not feeling 2 good. Had 2 ring Steve! Dinner sounds perfect.

RHYS: Cool. I tried 2 tell u, I begged u not 2 take her back with u. Knew u wud regret it

I slowly open the bathroom door and risk a glance out. Looks all clear. Thank God blondie has left. I walk over to the bed and see a note lying there.

> *Really enjoyed last night Jax. You definitely know how to show a girl a good time. So sad you can't spend the day in bed with me today but we will have to meet up. Ring or text me anytime xoxoxoxox*

I see her number at the bottom near a lipstick kiss. I chuck it in the bin, I will not be getting in touch with her again.

Chapter 2

Kendal

"Wakey wakey! Wakey wakey! Wakey wakey"

I wake up to Finley shouting and jumping on my bed. Every bounce makes the bed dip, taking me with it. Not a good way to wake up, but this is my daily wake up call.

"Fin please stop jumping."

Finley ignores me and carries on jumping and laughing at me.

"Okay Fin, I'm up."

He takes one last bounce and lands on his bottom.

"Juice mummy."

Another morning routine for my son. When I'm finally awake, he quickly demands what his stomach wants.

"Yes, okay.."

I throw my dressing gown over my pajamas.

"Toast mummy."

I nod and watch him closely as he walks down the stairs.

"Biscuits mummy."

I set him down at the table while I fix his juice and toast with biscuits on the side. I turn on his cartoons, and I go about getting dressed for work. It looks sunny out, so I decide on my black pencil skirt and vest work top. As I'm walking down the stairs, all ready for work, I hear Finley's shouting from the kitchen.

"Oh no. Mummy! My juice!"

I rush down the rest of the stairs, and when I reach the kitchen I nearly laugh at what I see. Finley's sitting in the middle of the table, with his toy cars scattered around him. His legs are covered with juice, I hide the smile and put on my mummy face.

"Finley. How many times have I said no climbing on the table?"

He hangs his head and it melts my heart, but I have told him not to climb on the table a lot of times. Finley is a good kid, but he can be very mischievous.

"I'm sorry mummy."

I walk up to the table and place my hand on top of his hair.

"That's okay rock star."

He beams up at me because I used his nickname. I pick him up, off from the table.

"Ugh all wet mummy!"

He looks down at his pajama trousers with a scrunched up nose.

"Come on, let's get you dressed."

For the past year, no matter what I pick out for him, he doesn't want to wear it. He loves to choose his own clothes so without even trying to decide his clothes for him anymore we hurry to his bedroom. Finley stands like the little rock star he is and looks at his clothes. When he's dressed and ready, a quick glance at the time and I see it's 08:30am. Right - we need to go.

After I have taken Finley to school, I pull up in the hotel car park, where Bianca told me to come and shake away the nerves that are creeping in. This is the best hotel in town, if there are any celebrities or wealthy people visiting, this is where they come. The part of London where I live is the nice, quiet part where there's more greenery and parks than buildings and traffic. It's not too far from it all though, only a short drive away. That's why it can be a popular place for celebrities to sneak away to. Some of the celebrities and the wealthy like the area that much they decide to live here. Behind the small town and parks, about twenty minutes from my house, is where the big houses all are, tucked away for privacy.

I get out my car with my supplies and make my way to the hotel's huge glass front doors. I can't help but feel very out of place here. I hope that my client isn't stuck up.

After dealing with a very snooty receptionist, I step out of the elevator and into a very large corridor. I'm on the top floor, which means Sophie James must be rich to be able to afford one of the best rooms the hotel has to offer.

I knock on the large black door and it opens to a very pretty girl who looks about my age, she smiles back at me. She has long black hair, hazel eyes and is petite. She has a gorgeous tiny frame and large boobs, which are big enough to compete with Maisy's. Sophie looks like the kind of girl you hope is a bitch, just so you have a reason to hate her.

"Hi, are you Sophie James?"

She flashes a big white smile and nods.

"Yes hi, I'm sorry I had you come here. I don't know where everything is and my boyfriend hasn't had time to show me around yet."

"No, that's fine. I'm Kendal."

I hold out my hand for her to shake, but she surprises me by going in for a hug. She breaks away, slightly blushing.

"Oh, I'm sorry about that. I haven't been around girls for a while. I've been surrounded by my boyfriend and his friends for so long I miss having a girl to talk to."

She giggles away her awkwardness and leads me into her luxury hotel room. The fancy furniture complements the dark floor, the far wall is pure glass, showcasing a pretty view of my home city. Sophie leads me to a large white table facing the glass window.

"Is this okay?"

I nod and place my little case down on the floor as she offers me a cup of tea.

After telling me what she wants done to her hair, I get my nail examples out to show her a few ideas to look at while I'm busy cutting. We continue chatting while I style her hair. I'm surprised that we have a lot in common, and she seems like a cool chick. I can tell she has missed female chatter because the conversation with Sophie doesn't stop. I was afraid that I was going to have someone stuck up but she seems so nice. We laugh about everything, I'm shocked I've only known her for about an hour.

"I love the color of your hair, Kendal. I'd be too scared to dye my hair a color like that."

My hair is a plum color, and I love it. It's been this color for two years now. After I had Finley, began my new job, and started to move on with my life, I decided I needed a change and had Tanya to dye it for me. Jax loved my red hair and every time I looked in the mirror I would be reminded how much I missed him.

"Thanks, it was bright red before."

"You're brave, I don't think I would have the guts. I bet being a hairdresser does that to you."

"Honestly, being a hairdresser makes you more scared I think."

I go to find my mirror so she can have a look at her hair.

"So do you like it here?"

I turn around with the mirror in hand and see Sophie nodding and smiling at me.

"I'm moving here actually. My boyfriend's from around here and he wanted to move back. We're staying in the hotel until we can find a home."

Looking at the hotel they're staying in, I bet they're checking out the big houses that are hidden away, rather than a house like mine.

"Well I love living here, so I'm sure you will too."

She nods as I walk to her and open the mirror to show her. She gasps and fluffs her hair. We talk the entire time I do her nails and we're laughing again before we know it. You wouldn't have guessed we only just met. It's like we have known each other for years. It reminds me of how I clicked with Tanya when we first met.

"Erm, Kendal? I know we've only just met, but I like you and I don't get a lot of girly time. Will you come to lunch with me sometime? Bring a friend? I know it's weird, but I want to meet some new girlfriends seeing as I'm moving here."

I stop packing my tools away and look at Sophie, who's staring at her drying nails, looking a little nervous.

"I'd like that. Actually, how does Saturday sound? My friend Tanya was asking about having a lunch together, and I think you will fit in fine with them."

She looks up at me with a huge smile.

"That's perfect. I can't wait."

Chapter 3

The girls can't wait to meet Sophie, so we arranged to meet on Saturday at a cute little restaurant called Summers. It's a restaurant / tea room, somewhere we can't take Sam, James, and Mark. I think every girl should have close girlfriends. I don't know what I would do without my friends. They have helped me a lot over the past four years. While I'm going to be catching up with my girls, Finley will be with the guys at the local football match.

"Finley, Uncle Sam is here."

I'm about to walk to the door to unlock it for Sam, but Finley barges past me and beats me to the door. I grab the keys and walk towards a bouncing Finley. Christ, it's only a football match! As soon as the door swings open, Finley runs out to Sam, who has his arms open wide. He spins him around a few times and settles him down. I'm feeling guilty again just watching them

"You ready pal?"

"Yeah!"

"Alright, say bye to mummy and we will go."

Finley gives me a tight hug and a big sloppy kiss and I watch him walk away, he looks so damn cute. I can't help thinking that should be Jax holding his hand.

I wave bye to my baby and check my appearance before I leave. I'm in my navy blue figure hugging dress that stops just above the knees. My cream heels look great and I'm holding a cream bag to match. My hair is in a side fishtail braid. My make up is freshly done, I went with my usual cat eyeliner flick on my eyes and I'm all set to go.

As soon as I walk into Summer's, I spot Sophie sitting in a booth at the back. When she notices me, she stands up and gives me a warm hug. I hope she's going to like the girls because they can get a bit loud and carried away once we get into things. Who am I kidding? I can get loud and carried away once we get into things! I guess I'd better warn her.

"Don't worry, sounds like your friends are just what I need. I can't wait to meet them."

Well, that's a relief. Right on cue, my beautiful best friend walks in. I stand to give her a hug, and I introduce Sophie and Jessica to each other.

"Oh my god, Sophie! I love your shoes."

Jessica is a sucker for shoes and Sophie's wearing a stunning pair of red bottoms that has Jessica drooling. Just like that, they click and chatter away, bonding as if they've been friends for years. Not long after, Tanya and Maisy join us and they hit it off with Sophie just like Jessica. We're all blending together nicely, and Sophie's laughing away as we listen to each other's gossip and we fill Sophie in on some messy experiences.

"So girls, how did you meet?"

They all look to me, I suppose I did bring Tanya, who then brought Maisy.

"Well, to cut long story short, Jess and I met when we were ten and have been best friends ever since. We moved to the same school at twelve. We knew Mark from primary school, so he became our protective figure amongst the bigger kids. Mark joined the school's football team where he met Sam and James and three of us became five. All through school, Jess and Sam flirted but they didn't get together until after we left school. When I started the second year of my hairdressing course, I met Tanya. Tanya brought along Maisy one day and that's it. We've been like this for four years."

"That's a sweet story."

"And then Kendal had an appointment with you, Sophie and here you are, part of the gang too."

Sophie grins at Jessica.

"Thanks Jessica."

I'm glad the girls like Sophie as much as I do. She tells us she has been with her boyfriend, Reece for three years. You can tell she's in love with him. We talk about dirty things, nice things, funny things, and good old gossip. After dinner and a few drinks, I glance at my phone and notice the time. Jessica and I need to get back soon to meet Sam and Finley. Before I can say anything, Maisy slams her empty glass down and excuses herself.

"Well my sexy sisters, I have a date tonight, so I gotta love ya and leave ya."

Tanya says her goodbyes too and follows Maisy out, grilling her all the way. Whenever it comes to men or sex talk Tanya's always there trying to get every tiny detail. Sophie gives Jessica and me a hug goodbye.

"I've had a lot of fun today, you girls are a laugh. I have a date with Reece tonight so I'd better head back and get ready. We have to get together again."

Jessica and I drive separately, when we get to our street I pull up in front of my house and walk to Jessica's. It's only five minutes around the corner, I see all of the guys cars are parked in front. When I walk into the house I can hear a lot of shouting, I see Jessica looking into the living room. I stop beside her and see the reason for all the noise. The guys all mumble their hellos without looking up, they're sitting on the floor with little Finley playing Xbox. Poor Finley's car keeps bumping into the side, but I'm guessing he thinks he is another car because he's shouting and laughing.

"I'm winning! I'm winning!"

James looks over to Finley and smiles.

"Yeah Fin, you're beating everyone!"

It makes me smile, Jessica and I leave them to it and go into the kitchen. When I sit down at the table Jessica is staring at me.

"You want some tea?"

"Sure."

She quickly goes about making us some tea and then sits down, turning towards me.

"Okay, what do you need to tell me?"

Dammit, she knows me too well.

"You can tell me."

I sigh and look back up at her. I need to tell her.

"I've been doing some thinking lately."

She lifts that damn eyebrow at me, telling me to continue.

"I've been thinking about Jax, and if I made a mistake."

Both of Jessica's eyebrows shoot up and her face is shocked.

"For how long?"

I shrug and let it all go.

"Whenever Finley makes me proud, happy, or sad. The little things too, like telling me he loves me, or when I take him to school, or play football on the field. It all makes me feel guilty as hell Jess. I think that Jax should experience what I do every day, and I took that away from him. I wanted what was best for everyone, I wanted Jax to have his dream, I didn't want to keep him from that. I feel as if I've failed everyone, especially Finley. He needs his dad. I don't know what to do."

My voice cracks and a few tears escape. Jessica pulls me into a tight hug and smooths my hair.

"Everything's going to be okay. You know what I'm going to say, don't you?"

Yeah, I know what she's going to say. She thought I was making a huge mistake walking away from Jax, and an even bigger one by not letting him I was pregnant. She let me know right from the start that she didn't like what I was doing. She still stood by me to support me, no matter what.

"You broke that man's heart, Kendal. That day you broke both of your hearts."

"He would have gotten a normal job to support us and left his dream, Jess. I couldn't let him do that. I did't want him to resent Finley or me."

"Jax wouldn't do that to you and you know it. He would have thought of something. What are you gonna do now?"

I shake my head, I have no idea.

"Do you have any way of getting in touch with him?"

"No."

We sit in a comfortable silence while we drink tea.

Ten minutes later, the noise in the next room has stopped and they all stroll into the kitchen. Jessica and I have already eaten and the guys had their own dinner after the football game, so we finish the day with one of Jessica's homemade desserts. She owns a bakery and everything she makes is delicious. We all wolf it down and James breaks the silence after his bowl is empty.

"Have any of you seen the paper today? How mad is that-"

"No we haven't James!"

Sam growls at James from across the table, glaring at him. Something's going on here, but I'm not sure what. Nobody has looked at me yet but I have the feeling they don't want to. Finley laughs and points at James.

"Hahahahahaha! Uncle Sam shouted at you!"

He's still giggling and I see Jessica's mouth lift slightly at the corner. Everyone else still hasn't spoken or looked my way. Something's not right, I want to go home, I'm not going to be around them while they're acting like this.

"Okay.......well, it's getting late and I need to get Finley to bed."

Finley's laughter immediately stops, and he frowns at me.

"Ohhhhh but I'm not tired!"

I stand up, take Finley's hand in mine, and say our goodbyes.

When I get into bed I can't stop thinking about my friends. What was that all about? I get the feeling Sam didn't want me to know what James was going to say, but he only mentioned the paper. I open my bedside drawer, reach for my iPad and search the local paper's website. When the page finally loads, I get sweaty and my breathing becomes erratic. There's one photo of Jax and Leo walking out of the airport together, one of Rhys and Max on their phones, and another one showing them all getting into a car. I tear my eyes from the photo of Jax and read.

Decoy Returns Home

A source revealed that all four members of the world famous rock band, Decoy are missing their hometown. They are supposedly in the process of purchasing real estate and plan to set up roots in this city. They're said to be taking a well earned break after their worldwide tour. We're pleased to welcome Decoy back home and we can't wait for their performance at the annual Summer festival.

I drop the iPad onto the bed and drop my head into my hands. I try and hold back my tears, but it's obvious I can't. Is this for real? What if he sees Finley and me before I get a chance to explain?

I can't stop shaking. If Jax or one of his friends sees me with Finley, they will know who his dad is because they look so much alike. If he's really back, there's no question about it. I will have to tell him.

I feel hurt that my friends didn't tell me. This was obviously the reason behind the scene at Jessica's. Didn't they think I needed to know about this? The thought of maybe seeing Jax again has my heart hurting. Even the thought of bumping into Leo, Max, or Rhys has me in knots. They were great friends and it hurt to lose them too. I pick up my phone, I click on Jessica's number and wait for her to pick up.

"Kendal?"

She sounds a little hesitant, she knows why I'm calling.

"Why didn't you tell me?"

She huffs into the phone.

"I just didn't know how to tell you, I couldn't upset you. You seem happy, and this is just going to set you back again. If Fin wasn't in the next room, I would have told you today. I found out just before we met with Sophie. We decided to keep quiet until you said something. I thought that's what you were going to say earlier. Sam didn't want James upsetting you in front of Finley. I'm sorry, honey."

It's my turn to huff now. I was angry with her and just like that, it's gone. I can understand the position she was in. I'm still annoyed at how they all baby me.

"Fucking hell Jess, what am I going to do?"

"You should try and tell him before he finds out for himself, especially if he has moved back here."

I'm pretty sure that between the girls and his money, he's living a very happy life. I bet he doesn't even think about me and thanks me for letting him go so he can enjoy his stardom. The thought really hurts, but I chose this, so I have to live with it. I know Jessica is right. I do need to tell him, but how and when? I've kept this a secret from Jax for four years. It's going to be hard to come clean.

Chapter 4

Jax

I look around the empty house. It's a family's dream the problem is, I don't have a family. This is more Rhys' style since he's settling down with his girlfriend. As I look out over the huge garden, my phone vibrates. It's Leo.

"Yeah?"

"Jax, have you found a place yet?"

"Nope."

"Max and I might have a solution."

"Go on."

"We've just signed the contract for this three bedroom house near where Rhys is moving. We can split the rent if you want?"

Max and Leo were looking to get something together. I wanted some peace and quiet. Could I share a house with them? They're great guys and we've been best friends since teenagers. However, after months of being on a tour bus with them, I could kill them.

"Look, just come and have a look yeah? Then you can make your mind up."

True, I don't see why not. If it's big enough, I suppose I could stay with them for a while. Besides, a house has more room to get away from them than a tour bus, right?

Five minutes later, I pull up to the address Leo gave me. I follow the dirt road and I'm shocked when I see the house. I step out of my car, and Max opens the front door.

"Welcome to our home!"

As soon as I enter the house we're in the living area. There are enormous glass panel windows that brightens the room. On the other side is a huge kitchen area, with only a wall separating it from the living and dining areas. One wall is just glass with patio doors in the middle to let you out to the garden. We walk out the patio doors and I spot Leo walking towards us with a huge grin on his face."So Jax, what do ya think of this place?"

"Looks cool. It's pretty big. What's in there?" I point to the outhouse where Leo came from.

"Pool table, arcade games, there's even a bar!"

The guys take me back inside and make our way back through the kitchen and living room. We enter a door near the front and a huge empty room obviously designed to be a movie room.

"I think we should use this as a second living room. We need space from each other, and we might not always want to watch the same shit on TV."

I'm impressed by Max, he makes a good point and I'm already warming to the idea of moving in. The guys lead me up stairs, they show me their rooms and the bathroom.

"I know we aren't the easiest people to live with, so when we saw this house's little secret, we knew you had to have it."

He opens the last door and lets me walk in first. I climb some stairs and when I reach the top, I'm shocked. This room is huge and has its own bathroom. The coolest thing is the glass doors leading to my own balcony. I can see over the garden, but it is on the other side so I do not see the pool and the jacuzzi. This is definitely my room. I turn and see the guys looking back at me. Leo has a big smile on his face, he knows I'm going to say yes.

"Soooooooo?" I give them a nod and they high five each other. "Yes! Just think of all the pussy parties we can have man!"

I cringe. "You can count me out of the parties."

Leo rolls his eyes."We know, why do you think we let you have the best room in the house?"

Kendal

Two months later...

I'm sitting in the staff room at work with Tanya and she's talking about the shopping trip she has arranged. Apparently she has no clothes.

After her talking stops I welcome the silence and daydreaming.

Will Jax be happy that he has a son? He's bound to get angry with me. Will he forgive me? I do feel shitty about the whole thing and yes, I know I did this, but I thought I was doing the right thing. Now I think I made the wrong choice. It's hard because four years ago, I made this immense decision. I thought I was doing what was best for everyone. Jax gets his dream, and I wouldn't get the blame keeping him from it, but poor little Finley is losing out. I've not heard anything more about Decoy, so until then I don't know what to do.

"I think I might buy a vibrator."

I was way in too deep with my thoughts that Tanya's made me choke on my tea.

"I'm sick of men. They think they're great in bed, and when it gets down to business they're a bag of shit. They just take care of themselves and do not even let you finish. Selfish bastards."

I laugh as I clean myself up. "You're just looking at the wrong guys. You always go for the bad boy look so look elsewhere."

"True, but when you have a gorgeous male there, and he's telling you all these things he could do to you that I so badly want I crave. Ever since that hook up four years ago the sex is shit and it is pissing me off."

Ah, the mysterious hook up. We don't know his name because Tanya won't tell us, so he's known as "the hook up".

One night we all went out together, us and the band. The next morning Tanya was in a fabulous mood. Apparently she met someone, he was extremely good in bed and gorgeous too. She must have met this guy after a Decoy gig because she disappeared and turned up an hour later in a foul mood, so we left. I think the excellent sex guy turned out to be a jerk, and she wouldn't tell us anything more. It didn't stop her from still sneaking out to see him though.

Four years later and she still won't tell us who he was. Sex has never been the same for poor Tanya. That guy ruined her for other men, a bit like how I feel about Jax.

"And do these guys do all these things they say?"

"They try but they're shit."

A week later...

It's Tuesday. The night before the girly shopping trip and the gang is at Sam and Jessica's house. Sadly, Sophie couldn't make it because she had to attend a work event with Reece, her boyfriend. We're having a great family meal. That is until Tanya lets slip that she wants a vibrator. I immediately drop my knife and fork to cover Finley's little ears and stare daggers at her from across the table. The guys are all shaking their heads, but Mark looks disgusted.

"Why the hell would you want one of those things?"

Tanya looks at him like he's crazy for asking such a question. To be honest I'm with Tanya there. Isn't it obvious why she would want one?

James shakes his head. "It's not the real thing, surely it doesn't feel the same. Get a man and do it with the real thing."

All the girls including me all gasp at James. I can't believe he just said that.

"Every girl should have one to be honest." Everyone stops to gawk at Maisy and she just shrugs her shoulders. She looks around the table at each of our stunned faces. "What? A girl has needs, with a vibrator there's no relationship crap."

The silence is filled with our laughter until Finley asks everyone a question I was dreading.

"What's a vibrator?"

Everyone looks at each other in a panic.

"Ermmm....It's a toy that Tanya really wants for her birthday but we can't say that word again or she won't get her birthday wish."

I hear Jessica snicker under her breath beside me. "She sure wants that birthday wish."

That over, we all start on the delicious double chocolate fudge cake Jessica had made. Maisy asks the guys what they have been up to lately. All three of them shift in their chairs a little, looking a little nervous. James shrugs his shoulders. "Just the usual boring stuff."

The girls all exchange looks. They're hiding something. "And that would be?"

His eyes shoot up to meet mine. Something's up, I can feel it. Tanya narrows her eyes at the guys. "Come on, what is it?"

Jessica's slowly nodding, looking straight at Sam but Sam has his head down on his bowl. The guys then all look to each other and it looks like Sam has the unfortunate responsibility of spilling the details. Weirdly he looks directly at me. "We just went to the new casino opening that's just outside of Chelsea."

Okay, well that's not so bad. "So what happened? You lose a lot of money or something?" Jessica points right at Sam. "Samuel Mathews, you're acting weird. Tell me now or so help me."

He bows his head and takes a big breath. I'm feeling nervous. Finley is oblivious to it all and takes advantage by snatching my bowl of cake.

"Sam!"

He snaps his head up and looks up to the ceiling. "OK fine. But just so you know, we did want to tell you but we didn't know how."

All three men look at me as Sam carries on talking. What is happening here?

"We were there for a couple of hours when we bumped into Max and Leo."

Oh shit. I think I felt my heart stop beating. I feel sick. I feel everyone's eyes on me but I'm looking at Finley. I hear Jessica's quiet voice. I tell Finley to go and play outside with Sam and Jessica's puppy. He happily agrees and runs out to the back garden. As soon as he is outside, I look up at the guys.

"So it's true. They really are back?"

My voice comes out as a whisper, Mark's the only one who nods "Looks that way, we spoke for a while and left."

Tanya grabs my hand from under the table and squeezes.

"What did they have to say?"

"They just said hi, they have a place about twenty minutes away from town."

He goes quiet and scratches the back of his head. A nervous gesture of his. "They said they share the place with Jax."

My stomach wants to reject the food I just enjoyed. Jax sharing a place with Leo and Max? The same guys who would shag any woman who offered? I bet they have women over all the time. See, Kendal who? Jax is happy without me, I did do him a favor running from him.

"Who's Jax mummy?" Finley's sweet little voice interrupts my panic. He's standing at the back door, chocolate all over his face. I try to smile and force back the tears.

"Mummy's old friend, sweetheart. Come on, it's time to go home."

"But I don't want to mummy."

Jessica stands behind my chair and whispers in my ear. "He can stay with us tonight if you want?"

I appreciate the offer, but the truth is I feel like I need Finley with me at the minute. "No. I need him with me. I just need to go."

As soon as Finley and I get inside, we go straight upstairs. I finish reading Finley his bedtime story and set it back on his shelf. "Mummy?"

I smooth down his messy hair. "Yes?"

"Who is Jax?"

My hand pauses on his hair, and I bite my lip. "You remember when mummy said that your daddy lives far away?" He nods his head, and I get myself together. I have to tell him. "Well, Jax is your daddy baby."

I see him take this in, and he yawns. "Did he make you cry?"

"No honey he didn't make me cry, I cried because I miss him."

"You miss daddy?"

I gulp. I didn't think I'd be talking about this with Finley for a while yet. "Yes I miss your daddy Finley. Maybe we will see him again."

He nods at me with a big smile and his eyes roll and his lids look heavy. I stroke his hair and his breathing slows and evens out. I remove my hand and sit and stare at my beautiful baby lying asleep. While I'm looking at him, I decide there and then I know I have to tell Jax. Finley does need his dad, and I can't hide the fact that I feel like I need him too. I have help from my friends and my parents, but I suppose it is different when the father of your child helps. I lie down next to Finley and cuddle up to him. I whisper, so I don't wake him up.

"I will try and fix this, I promise."

I kiss him on his head and snuggle in closer.

Chapter 5

After I take Finley to school I drive straight to Tanya's. Despite what happened at dinner last night, I feel okay. I think that little talk with Finley before bed helped. When I pull up outside Tanya's apartment I buzz her door number on the intercom

"Hello?"

"Tan, it's me."

"Eager beaver. Come on up."

She buzzes me in, and I walk through the apartment lobby to the elevator. Tanya lives in a very nice small block of modern apartments. They're only five floors high, Tanya lives at the top. When I get to her door Tanya already has it open.

"So you're early."

We walk down her bright hallway barefoot on her light wooden floor.

"I came straight from school."

"No prob, you want a cuppa?"

"Please."

I sit down at her stylish breakfast bar. While the kettle boils she rests her elbows on the bar right in front of me and quirks her eyebrow. "How you feeling?"

"I said no talking about that."

She pouts and walks away to finish our drinks. "Oh come on Kendal. I won't be able to ask you when Sophie gets here."

"I'm OK Tan, don't worry. Oh, by the way I told Finley last night that

Jax is his dad."

She stops what she's doing and turns to look at me, her eyebrows high on her forehead. "You did?"

"He asked who Jax was when I took him to bed, I couldn't lie to him Tan. He thinks he lives far away."

"Well until a few weeks ago, he probably did." She sets my drink down in front of me. "What are you going to do? Are you going to try and find him?"

"I don't know. I want to, but I'm scared shitless. I don't know how he's going to react. He has a right to get mad at me. I carried his baby and kept Finley a secret and he's turning four this year. It's my fault he doesn't even know his son. I'm an awful person and an evil mother."

Tanya slams her cup on the breakfast bar making her tea spill. I look up at her in shock. Tanya walks around to my side of the breakfast bar looking pissed. "Don't you dare say that shit. You're the fucking best mum I know. You did what you thought was right! To be honest, if I were you, I think I would have done the same." She grabs me into a big hug. "Don't you dare talk shit like that. You are everything to that little boy."

She kisses my cheek, and we break apart. She sits down on the stool beside me. "You still love him, don't you?"

I take a sip of my tea.

"Do you still love Jax?"

"Yes! I haven't seen him for four years, and I still love him. Stupid, silly old Kendal crushing on Jax Parker just like his fans."

"You're not at all like a fan, you two have history and he's the father of your child. I don't think it's stupid that you still love him. I knew that's why you ended it with Harley. I thought you were mad at first, I mean who would not want that piece of ass?"

I love how Tanya can turn a serious conversation around and make me laugh. She understands I don't want to talk about it anymore. Instead she asks for juicy details on comparisons between Harley and Jax in bed. Not long after Maisy and Jessica arrive, I notice they both squeeze me tighter than what they normally do. All of our phones beep text messages.

SOPHIE: *Just leaving. I have exciting news!*

Maisy tilts her head to the side. "Huh. I wonder what the news is."

Tanya gasps. "She's pregnant!"

Could be, but I don't think it is. Five minutes later Tanya disappears into her living room and we hear her shout."Oh my god guys! Come here!"

Tanya's looking out of the window from her living area. We all follow her gaze and my eyes widen. Sophie is standing by a black Range Rover and kissing the driver which is obviously Sophie's boyfriend.

"Fucking hell Sophie's boyfriend is loaded." Tanya gives us an excited look."I wonder if he has sexy rich friends!"

Jessica places her hands either side of Tanya's face and leans in close."Don't ask Sophie anything about her boyfriend's money, or his rich friends."

"But-"

"No."

"Yeah but h-"

"Tanya!"

Tanya huffs and stomps over to buzz Sophie into the apartment building. As soon as Sophie steps in Tanya pounces."Sooo, what's this news then?"

Sophie beams at us all."I will tell you when we get something to eat. I'm starving."

Tanya groans."Aww, Sophie you're killing me."

We all laugh as we make our way outside and get into my car. At the front of the shopping center there's a cute little cafe so we all head in and as soon as we sit it's Maisy who pounces on Sophie this time. "Sooooo?"

"Alright I'll tell you. I can't hold it in any longer." The waitress approaches and after we've ordered and she leaves we loo to Sophie."Reece planned a surprise on Monday. He wouldn't tell me where we were going and when I got into his car, he pulled out a blindfold."

Tanya gasps loudly."Why?"

Jessica turns to Tanya and rolls her eyes. "Will you let the girl talk so she can tell us."

"He didn't want me to see where we were going. When the car stopped he helped me out the car and buckled me into a seat."

This time it's Jessica who gasps but nobody says anything.

"A while later we stop and again he helped me outside and puts me into another car. We drive for a few minutes and when we stopped walking he finally took off the blindfold and I was speechless. We were outside in the dark, in front of us is a small table with lit candles, the stars are out and I'm surrounded by white twinkling fairy lights. We sit down and waiters appear from nowhere bringing us our food. Then, as I'm looking around I realize where I am. He took me to Paris!"

We all gasp, he blindfolded her and took her on a surprise meal to fucking Paris! I need a man like that! I look at the girls and they're all wide eyed and shocked just like me.

"Yeah, I know but it's not just that. I look around and it hits me, I'm on the Eiffel Tower!"

"He took you for a meal on the Eiffel Tower? Oh my god, I need a Reece."

"After we finished our dinner Reece took me over to the railings to look at the view. He says my name from behind and when I turn around he's down on one knee."

"Oh my God!"

"Shut up"

"Where is the ring?"

I laugh at the girls."Congratulations Sophie. I'm so happy for you!"

She reaches in her bag and takes out a little black box and pulls out a huge diamond ring. Nobody even bothers looking away as our food is placed on the table. "The wedding is in two months."

We all gawp at her. I decide to ask her, "Why that quick?"

"Reece might have to go away in a few months for work again but we want to be married before he does. We've been together for three years and I know I want to be his wife so why wait? We've even found our perfect home and we move in next week."

After the good news we start our girly day spending money. Before we go home, we enter a sex shop. Maisy is the only one of us who has a vibrator so she helped Tanya. We couldn't stop laughing at all the sex toys and Sophie looked afraid of some of them so Sophie, Jessica an I waited outside.

It's 2:00pm when we get back to Tanya's apartment, we all have a much needed cup of tea after a hard day of shopping. We're sitting in Tanya's living area when Sophie groans."Will you girls please make sure none of the stuff in that sex shop makes an appearance on my hen do? I hate all that stuff."

Tanya looks shocked."What? Really? No cock straws? No blow up man with a hard on? No strap ons? No-"

Sophie holds her hands out in front of her. "No! God please no!"

Maisy sits forward on her place on the sofa. "So, we're going to your hen do?"

Sophie looks around at us all."What? You didn't think you were coming? Of course you're all coming! In fact I want you all to plan it for me as a surprise. Any money you need let me know how much and I'll hand it over, there's no need for you to pay."

"You want us to plan it?"

Sophie looks to Tanya. "Obviously, you're my best friends. That's your job when your best friend gets married. I can't believe you all thought you weren't coming! Actually, I have another thing to ask."

She looks serious. Sophie takes her time smiling at us all. "I was wondering, if you would all like to be my bridesmaids?"

By our sudden jumping and squealing I think she took that as a yes.

"It will just be us. Reece's sister in-law can't make it and I don't want my mum there. She's too uptight to come. My mum has planned a family meal for me, so you all need to plan a fun hen."

I take Sophie back to her hotel in my car. I have to go that way to get Finley from school. "I'm really happy for you Sophie."

"I'm glad you can all be my bridesmaids. Reece is a bit nervous because he hasn't met you all yet so I guess we need to plan that."

"Yeah, I guess we do need to meet him before the wedding."

"I would like that. There's also someone else I would like to meet."

I raise my eyebrows at her, who else would she want to meet? She's met the guys.

"Finley."

Oh shit, I didn't even think about that. How stupid of me, she's one of my best friends. Of course she wants to meet my son. I've managed to keep it a secret this long but I don't think I can hide him for much longer.

"Of course, sorry I didn't even think about that! Well, I guess we can all meet together. A meal maybe? Reece can come, and Finley, I'll ask the guys."

She gives me a big smile. "Great."

After fetching Finley from school we go to my parents for dinner. When we have all finished our dinner, dad and Finley are in the living room while I'm helping my mum clean up.

"Everything okay honey?"

"Fine, why?"

"Finley said you were shouting at Sam. He also told me you were crying."

When did he say this?

"I'm fine mum, we just had a fall out. No problem, it's all forgotten."

"And who is Jax?"

My heart drops. Shit.

"Look, I told him his dad's name OK?"

"Then why did Fin say Jax made you cry?"

Dammit! Finley listened and saw more than I thought.

"He said that?"

She puts down her towel and takes hold of my hand and pulls me out to the garden.

"Now I know what you've told me but I don't believe you Kendal. Finley told me and your father that Jax made you cry because you miss him. Now I know you wouldn't act like that over someone you just spent a weekend with and I also remember Jax was the name of that older boy you were seeing when you were at college."

Fuck! Fuck! Fuck!

"You sure you don't know where he is?"

"No and that's the truth. I do think Finley should know his father. Until I can figure out this mess, can you not say anything more, please?"

She bites her bottom lip and then nods.

"Don't expect me to be happy about this."

That night when I'm in bed I get my laptop and do something that I haven't done for about two years. I load up YouTube and type *Decoy* into the search bar. I see their music videos and interviews. At the top of the list there's a freeze frame picture of Jax, it's an interview from last week. I click it and I can't help but marvel at how sexy he is. His black hair is in its usual messy style. He has a slight shadow of stubble, which makes him look rough and ready. His dark eyelashes make his gray eyes pop out. He has a tight black shirt on and his shoulders look huge. He starts talking, his voice sounds amazing, deep and manly.

"So Jax, Decoy's new single Never Let Go is released this weekend. The fans seem to love it, can you tell us what inspired the song?"

Jax grins at the interviewer but I can tell he's nervous because he twiddles with his earlobe, his nervous habit.

"Sure, the song is all about a girl who has a hold of your heart but one day you lose her. Your heart still bleeds for her. You try to move on but no other girl will ever compare so you can, Never Let Go."

He glances to the camera and my heart skips.

"The record label said you wrote this song. Is this from personal experience?"

Jax just grins at the interviewer and shuffles a little in his seat.

"Let's just say I can never let go of mine."

I shut my laptop before I can hear anymore. Oh my god, could he be talking about me? I couldn't affect him like that, could I? It's me who can't get over him. He's famous now, he's forgotten all about boring old me.

I get into my bed and try my best not to think about those haunting gray eyes staring at me, and his last words 'I can never let go of mine'.

Chapter 6

Over the next six days it's the usual routine for me. Take Finley to school and go to work.

The best days are when I have a day off work at the weekend so Finley and I have the whole day together.

Sophie has arranged a bridesmaids' dress fitting today for us. Maisy has been very excited because Sophie told us that the designer, Gloria Stevens, is sending dresses for Sophie to choose from. Maisy is not just crazy about house design, she loves clothing designs too. So trying on exclusive dresses from Gloria Stevens is a big deal to Maisy.

I'm excited to finally see Sophie's new house. She text us her address and I've just arrived. Well, I say arrived, but I'm not even on the property yet. Sophie's house is in one of the richest areas, of course. I'm sitting in my car in front of a set of huge gates. I roll down my window and press the buzzer. A minute later, Sophie's voice comes out the little speaker above the button I just pressed.

"Hey Kendal."

I look around the inside and outside of my car to see if she's there. How did she know it was me?

"How do you know it's me?"

She laughs and I hear Maisy.

"There's a camera above the gate you idiot."

"Come on in."

Sophie's still giggling when the gates open for me. I follow a little road that's surrounded by green grass and trees. The road leads me to the front of the house where there's a significantly large drive.

I spot Maisy's car and park next to it. By the time I'm out my car, I see Sophie and Maisy standing at the front door of the house. It's a huge place. Sophie gives me a hug and then leads me to the room where we will all be trying on our dresses. I try and look at as much of the house as I can.

When we enter a large room, which Sophie tells us is going to be her dining room, I see a cute girl who looks about eighteen on the other side talking on her phone. She offers a smile and a wave and carries on talking quickly to whoever is on the phone.

"That's Sarah, the girl I told you about. She works with Gloria and brought the dresses around. I think she's talking to Gloria on the phone now actually. She badly wants us to choose one of her dresses."

There's a beeping sound and Sophie rushes off, leaving me and Maisy alone with Sarah. A few minutes later Tanya appears in the room.

"Where's Sophie?"

"On the phone in the other room."

Tanya and Maisy ask me how I'm feeling. Tanya hasn't said anything about me confessing my love for Jax but right now I can see her concern written all over her face. Her eyes say it all. They are full of sympathy and sadness for me.

After a couple of minutes of mindless chatter, there's another beeping sound throughout the house and not long after Sophie comes back in with Jessica behind her. We quiz Sophie on any ideas she would like for her hen. We don't tell her that we were all at my house the other day talking about ideas about whisking her away for a couple nights for a hen weekend.

"Right girls, are we all ready?"

We turn at Sarah's chirpy voice. She is now off her phone and pulling the two racks full of dresses towards us. She then goes back and pulls another two so all four are all lined up. Each rack has each of our names on the front.

"Sophie sent me all your dress sizes and you all have the same dresses arranged in the same order. Now let's start trying these bad boys on."

We all look at each other as we're in the ninth dress we have tried on. They've all been beautiful dresses but only one so far has made Sophie's eyes get that little sparkle.

We're now in a pink dress. The top half is a boob tube style that pulls in which I love because it sucks in my little blob on the bottom of my stomach that no amount of sit ups will get rid of. I don't mind it that much to be honest. I have it because I have Finley. How can I be mad at that?

The bottom half of the dress is gorgeous. It has a lot of bling on the top and has a faded design, so as the sparkle reaches the bottom of the skirt there's hardly anything there. It puffs out too but not too much. The length rests above the knee but I'm not 100% on the top half. The sparkles don't fit in with it, but the skirt I love. We all look at each other and then towards Sophie. She has that twinkle in her eyes.

"You all look stunning. Sarah, do you have these in navy?"

"Yep, do you want the sashes that come with them?"

"No, I think they look better without."

Sophie stands looking at us frowning and tapping her chin while she thinks. "Something's missing. Sarah, do you think I could combine dresses?"

Combine dresses? This is interesting. Sarah now has her hands on her hips. "Maybe. What are you thinking?"

Sophie turns to the rack of dresses and fishes out the pale green dress we had tried on earlier. This dress is also a boob tube top and is covered in sparkles and the skirt is plain, not anything special. "I really like the top on this dress. It fits their bodies better and I think the sparkles match the skirt on the one they're wearing now better than the one it comes with."

Sarah smiles and walks away from the room dialing on her phone. I think about the bodice on the green dress we tried. The contrast from the all over sparkles to the faded out sparkle design on the skirt of the pink dress would look interesting.

We all change back into our clothes when Sarah strolls back into the room. "Well I just spoke to Gloria and told her your idea Sophie. She loved it."

Sophie looks shocked and her hands cover her mouth. "Seriously?"

"Yeah, she thinks it's a great idea. She's going to have them made for you. I just need all your correct measurements and we will have them made in the navy blue you want."

Sophie screams and jumps up and down on the spot clapping her hands."Oh my god! Thank you so much Sarah! They will look amazing; I can't wait to see them."

"That's not all, she also said she has the most amazing shoes to go with the dresses and will send them over with the dresses."

Sophie stands there, huge smile on her face and wipes the palm of her hand across her forehead."I can't believe it; you guys are going to look amazing."

She runs up to Sarah and throws her arms around her.

"Bridesmaids come and join in!"

We all run over, do a group hug and then laugh uncontrollably. The girls all stay and have drinks with Sophie but I have to leave so I can fetch my gorgeous little rock star.

Jax

I've been living with Max and Leo for two weeks now and they've had parties both weekends and a couple of times during the week. They're not the kind of social parties where you get drunk with your friends and have a good time. Max and Leo's parties only include girls and most of them are half naked. After the first party they had, I've not been to one since.

Today I finally traded in my rental and I bought myself a car. I want to buy the car I've wanted for years, a silver Aston Martin DB9. It's a beast and I spent all morning driving it around.

Right now, I'm trying to write some lyrics on the balcony of my room but Leo and Max are having another party. I didn't think living with them would be this bad. I understand that they're single and why there doing it but If I wasn't so fucking hung up on Kendal, then I would probably be down there with them.

I walk down the stairs from my room and lock the door behind me. After the first party I got locks on my door because the girls tend to wander off around the place. On the landing area, there's a big glass panel looking out to where the party is taking place. Even though it's getting dark, it is still hot. They are about ten girls in and beside the pool, all in barely there bikinis. Leo is happily sitting in between some girls on the side of the pool. Max is in the attached Jacuzzi with four girls, all with champagne glasses in their hands. Max is looking very pleased with himself. I've never been in the jacuzzi because of what I have seen in the past. One night, I came home from being with Rhys when I saw the patio doors open. I went to go and close them, but I saw Max and Leo having sex with some random girls while in the jacuzzi.

Since I woke in the hotel with the mystery blonde, I decided no more sex with groupies or any other girls. Over the past four years, I have had so many girls under me and at first it was exciting, but then it got old and boring. Obviously Max and Leo have no problem with having cheap meaningless sex. I hold nothing against them, let them have their fun, but it's not for me anymore.

I'm fed up, and I don't want to listen to the giggling girls or the music anymore, so I decide to get in my new DB9 and drive to nowhere in particular.

Fifteen minutes later, I'm in a quiet little part of town. It's pretty around here, parks and fields everywhere. I enter the local town and I'm pleased to see its quite empty seeing as it's getting dark now. I find a place where I can park, so I can walk and do some thinking. I grab my cap and shades so if I do see anyone hopefully they will not recognise me. I don't see anyone, so I'm free to let my thoughts run. I think about everything, but whatever I think about always comes back to Kendal, especially now that I'm back here in London where we first met. I think back on these past four years without her.   Yeah, I've had my career to keep me busy, but it's been pretty lonely.

One day I will have Kendal back. I know I will.

My phone beeps, gladly breaking me away from my desperate thoughts.

RHYS: *Hey man where R U? Max just rang asking if U were with me*

I'm surprised he realized I left.

ME: *Another fucking party. I'm just fucking about, can't deal with their shit anymore*

RHYS: *Fucking hell man! How many they gonna have? U can come over if U want, gym tomorrow?*

I reply back telling him I'm fine. I've been around his place far too much lately and I don't want to take advantage. Plus Rhys just proposed to his girlfriend and they're all happy and shit. The way I'm feeling now, I think I would only spoil their mood.

I do say yes to the gym though because lately the gym has been a good way to relieve stress.

Another thing I think over as I walk is my best man speech. Max and Leo have also been chosen as best men too, as well as Rhys' older brother Rex. Only me Rex and I are doing speeches. Can you imagine what Leo and Max would say? Rhys does not want that in front of his family.

I stop frozen on the path. There are a few couples walking around. One of the couples is two people I did not think I would see again. Walking hand in hand across the road is Sam and Jessica. I look around and it looks like they're on their own, I don't think they can see me though. I'm in the shadows of the trees near the park on the other side of the street. I think about going over to Jessica but I don't think I can. Kendal must still live in London if Jessica's here, because they will never leave each other. They were joined at the hip. I quietly watch Sam and Jessica enter a restaurant and I decide to go back home. I suddenly have the need to write down some lyrics.

Chapter 7

Kendal

One month later...

Finley and I keeping our same routine through another month. Sophie has happily settled in with all of us. She has made her own presence in the group as our enforcer. Sophie makes us all find the time to get together and we love her for it. We especially have a lot more girl time, which I cannot be happier about.

Jessica grabs my hand tightly and looks at me. She comes close to my face and says in a low voice, "Are you sure about this?"

I roll my eyes and sigh then push her away slightly. "Jess, you know how long I've wanted to do this. Now move so I can get in."

I barge past her and enter *Harleys Tattoos and Piercings*. I'm immediately hit by the smell of tattoos. I'm so fucking nervous to be here, and it's not because I'm having a new piercing. This is my ex-boyfriends business. I wouldn't have come here, but this is the only place I trust to get anything done.

When we enter, we're greeted by the receptionist. Harley must know I'm here; I have no clue how he's going to act.

Check in all done we go to sit on the red leather chairs.

Harley assured me by his last texts, after we broke up, that everything will be cool between us. I can't help but fight the need to run out of here. It's a shame that I couldn't have moved on with Harley. Women around the world will think I'm a mad woman. Wherever he goes women check him out, how could you not? Harley is one of those men who don't need to work out to get a fit body, he just has one. He screams sex with his muscled arms, tattoos and not forgetting that sinful V shape that leads to his delightful package. Jax has ruined me for all men. Harley may scream sex, but Jax is sex and much, much more! Plus there's the minor detail that I loved him and I think I still do as crazy as that sounds. I mean how can you get over an amazing man who you see on the TV, hear on the radio and see in magazines and papers. Jax knew how to treat me inside and out. He definitely knew how to treat my body. We had a raw connection that I know I will never have with anyone else. It was a huge bonus that his body looked like the body of a sculptured God. His arms, stomach and thighs were so toned. They didn't look anything like a boy. He was 100% man. That mouthwatering V was an open invitation to the rather large present in hiding. Although when we were alone it was never hidden. I spent a lot of time with that part of his body, it was practically my best friend and I loved it very, very much. God I miss my old best friend, a lot!

That's why I had to end it with Harley. I didn't realize he got so serious. My hearts breaking enough, I don't want to put anyone else through that pain.

"How are you feeling?" I look to Jessica who looks concerned. "Why don't you ask for someone else?"

"I think it's too late. He will know something's up if he hears me asking to have someone else."

I hear a door open and I snap my head up and see receptionist walking back to her desk with a folder and a pile of paperwork balanced on top. She huffs as she sits down. As I'm still looking at her, I don't see that Harley followed her out.

"Kendal?"

I snap my head in his direction; he's standing in front of the little hallway. He looks edible. This is not good. He's wearing slim black jeans and a tight black short sleeve top with his studio's logo on the front. He has his black biker boots on of course, because God forbid he doesn't already look sexy enough.

"Hi Harley."

He smiles that boyish smile. His left arm is covered in roses that I know continues all over onto his left peck. Harley steps closer, this is slightly awkward. I stand because I feel like I should, and I watch as his eyes drink me in from head to toe. I came here straight from my morning at work so I'm still in my uniform. He asks if Finley's okay and my heart warms at his question. He and Finley had a really good relationship. I reply and ask how he's doing and he gives me a nod with a lift of his eyebrow ."Better now I've seen you."

After Harley and Jessica have spoken, he turns his attention back to me. "Right then, please follow me."

Harley turns and walks off, not even looking to see if I'm following. I quickly look back to Jessica to see she's silently giggling at me so I give her the middle finger and hurry after Harley.

I sit down on a small leather chair in silence, already regretting coming here.

Harley gathers everything he needs and starts to ask me the necessary questions before a piercing."Finally brave enough to have your tongue done?"

I nod my head as he ticks away boxes and filling out some of my basic information. We were together for about a year, so I guess he knows nearly everything he needs for his form. I'm starting to feel really nervous around him, it's got to be Harley because I'm no stranger to piercings. I have my tragus, nose, and belly button pierced. Harley continues talking through all the safety and care for the new piercing and the risks. The usual stuff they have to say and I sign a form. I pick a simple gold bar for my tongue and he gets to work unpacking the new equipment.

"So I see you just came from work."

I look down at my uniform and scrunch up my nose. "I didn't have time to go change if I wanted to get Finley in time."

"I don't mind, I've always like your little uniform."

My little uniform? He makes it sound like I've dressed in some sexy little nurse's outfit for him.

"So, did you do the tanning course?"

I'm surprised he remembers. Around the time I ended things with

Harley, Bianca asked me if I minded doing a tanning course for her. I accepted. "Yep, so now I do everything."

Meaning work wise, but by the sparkle in Harleys eyes and the slight lift on the corner of his mouth, it tells me he's thinking of something else entirely. He always did have a dirty mind. He grabs my chair, which makes me jump a little. Harley pulls my little chair towards him, so my knees are touching his chair. He leans forwards and he's dangerously close.

"Right, let's get started shall we?"

I swallow hard and I think he heard it because I'm sure I saw him smirk before he turned away. He gets to work, and not long after I have my new piercing. When everything's all done, he stands and hands me some cleaning solution and heads towards the door. He places his big hand on the handle and turns towards me. "I'm sorry I fucked it all up."

I frown. Does he actually think that? Well, I didn't honestly go into detail when I called it quits."No, it wasn't you Harley. I'm just not in the right place."

Oh that felt weird talking. I can feel the tongue bar.

"So, one day you might be?"

I don't want to get his hopes up. I don't know, maybe I will manage to get over Jax. I really have no idea."I don't know Harley. It's hard, I'm sorry."

He reaches up and places his hand on my jaw. He rubs my cheekbone with his thumb."I want to wait for you. I miss you."

Oh no, I can't have him waiting. He misses me? I feel guilty as shit.

"No Harley. Please don't wait. I would hate myself if you did."

I look down at my shoes and feel awkward. I want to get out of here now. I feel his finger under my chin and he lifts my head so I'm looking right at him.

"Fine but I do miss you though."

Harley envelopes me in a hug and I welcome it. It feels so good to be hugged. It doesn't hurt that it's a big strong, sexy, man. I pull back and give him a smile that I hope looks like I'm okay. I walk out on my own and see Jessica looking through a black folder of tattoos. I quickly go to pay and walk out the building with Jessica right behind me.

"So, how was it?"

"It was okay, I didn't really feel it. It feels a bit sore now though."

She lightly smacks me on the side with the back of her hand."That's not what I asked and you know it."

"He was flirting a little but before I came out he ruined it. He told me he will wait for me and he misses me! I told him not to. God, I'm an awful person."

"No, you're not Kendal. What's not to miss about you? At least you were truthful and told him not to. It's not your fault."

I let her words calm me a little. I guess she's right.

***

At the kitchen table, I've finished my dinner and was surprised my tongue was OK. I'm watching Finley finish eating his spaghetti, he looks so funny. He's concentrating on picking up all the spaghetti and has a big orange circle around his mouth.

"So were you a good boy at school today?"

"Yes mummy."

"Good, tomorrow I was thinking if you wanted to we could go to the park?"

He slams his spoon and fork down and shouts. "Yeaaaahhh!"

I really do love my son. As I watch Finley I get that familiar stab of guilt in my heart. I feel selfish for having Finley all to myself. Jax should be feeling this too and it's my fault that he's not.

When Finley has finished his dinner and it's time for his bedtime I carry him upstairs. This little boy is my world and I'm scared I've done wrong by him.

When Finley's fast asleep I go back downstairs, clean up and settle down to watch some TV. When I see a text on my phone and see it is from Harley, I hesitate a little.

HARLEY: Hey Kendal its Harley. It was nice seeing u 2day. I'm sorry if I made u uncomfortable but it's true. I do miss u, cud we b friends? xxx

I stare at his text for a while, thinking of what I could reply. Could we be friends? I don't know, I would like to because I do actually miss his friendship. It was awkward for me today and weirdly he felt a little off.

ME: Yeah was good 2 c u 2. I think friends wud b nice but do u think that's a good idea?

HARLEY: I think friends wud b perfect, I do miss u Kendal, I miss talking 2 u and having a laugh. Maybe 1 day we cud meet up for dinner sometime and catch up. As friends?

I agree to meet up sometime but I don't know when that would be or if it's a good idea.

Chapter 8

"Wakey wakey! Wakey wakey! Wakey wakey!"

I don't even know why I bother setting my alarm. Finley manages to get up before its set to go off every morning. He's my alarm clock and there's no snooze button for Finley.

"Get up mummy!"

I grab my phone and wince when the screen wakes up and shines brightly in my eyes. I squint at the screen and manage to make out the time. It's 6:30! I roll onto my front and groan into the pillow like a teenager. Finley has outdone himself today.

"Come and have a cuddle with mummy."

He quirks his eyebrows at me like I'm crazy but he jumps under the covers with me. Finley giggles a little as he wiggles about to get comfy. I cuddle up to him and sigh deeply. Who needs a man when I have my little guy right here? Finley is everything I need.

"I love you buddy."

He squeezes me tightly with his tiny little arms."Love you mummy."

"Let's go back to sleep."

It's silent and I smile to myself thinking I've gotten away with it."Mummy, juice pleeease."

I inwardly groan. I should have known better.

"And biscuits."

I flip the covers off me and sit up.

"Please mummy."

"Yes OK Finley, let me go wee wee first."

I get up off my bed and begin to walk when a little blur of fast movement comes from beside me. Finley bounces off my bed and barges past me. "I go wee wee first!"

After we sit together for half an hour watching cartoons and eating our breakfast, I leave him to his toys while I get ready for work. I pick black shorts today with my purple Bianca's work top. Simple make-up with my usual cat eyeliner flick and I pull my hair up in a high, messy bun. I'm glad I'm not working a full day. I shout for Finley to come upstairs so he can pick out his clothes.

When I've only been at work for ten minutes Sally, another hairdresser, pokes her head around the staff room door."Hey Kendal, there's a sexy guy asking for you at the reception."

A sexy guy, who could that be? I thank her and think it could be Harley. He's the only sexy guy I know at the minute. I enter the reception area and see exactly who it is. I wouldn't choose the word sexy because I don't see him that way at all. I suppose if you didn't think of him as your brother you would think of him as sexy. Standing there with his dark blonde hair looking a mess is my close friend James. He's looking a bit rough at the minute. Wait, he's in a shirt and dark skinny jeans. Are those last night's clothes? Oh! Ew!

"Hey James, what's up?"

He smiles and gives me a quick kiss on the cheek."Can you talk?"

I look up at the clock. Maisy's not going to be here for 30 minutes. I nod and step out in front of the salon. He's looking anywhere but at me and I'm getting a sense of de-ja vu here and I don't like it. "James?"

"Yeah, erm." He scratches the back of his neck and looks straight at me. "Last time you were upset about us not saying anything, so I thought I'd just come and tell you straight away."

I roll my hand for him to carry.

"Right OK. Well I stayed out last night and I was just walking back when a guy was jogging towards me. He had his cap on low so I couldn't really see his face but when he came up close I saw exactly who it was. He knew who I was too."

"Who was it James?" I ask desperately.

"It was Rhys."

Oh fuck. Wait, didn't he talk to him?

"Where was this? Did you talk to him?"

"He was on that quiet road at the back of town. No, we didn't talk, it was pretty weird."

I give James a slight nod. I wish he could have spoken to him; I need a number or an address for Jax.

"Well, that's three out of the four of them. Jax is definitely here, if you see any of them again I need a number or something. Tell the guys for me?"

He frowns at me and just nods his OK."Are you going to finally tell him?"

I smile and nod my head yes."Thanks for letting me know."

"I didn't know whether to wait or not because you're at work, but I had to tell you. I felt like shit last time, and I think you're doing the right thing by the way. He needs to know."

He gives me a big hug, another kiss on the cheek and whispers he loves me. I watch him walk away before I go back into work.

I set up for when Maisy arrives. As soon as she sees my face, she knows something is wrong. I tell her everything that James told me. Maisy listens to every word I say and gives her input at appropriate times like a good friend."I suppose it's only a matter of time until one of us sets eyes on Jax now."

I smudge her nail art on her middle finger. Shit! She could have warned me she was going to come out with something like that.

"Oh shit, sorry Kendal, me and my big mouth. I didn't think I'm sorry."

I wish everyone would stop saying sorry and looking at me like I'm on my deathbed. I appreciate them being here for me and I feel really ungrateful, but I don't need them to pity me. It makes it too hard to cope.

"Maisy, it's fine, I wish you would all stop being so sensitive around me."

"We just don't know what to say honey, and then we don't know how you are going to react to what we say. We're just looking out for you, we're worried about you. This is a big thing."

Well, now I just feel like a piece of shit. She's right. I am being ungrateful thinking badly of their sympathy."I'm sorry, I just don't know what to do anymore. I'm shitting myself. I just want all of you to go back to normal, be yourself and that will actually help."

"I'm sure we can all do that."

I can't wait to finish work and spend the rest of the day at the park with my little boy.

***

"Mummy's home!"

I've only just taken off one shoe when two little arms wrap around one of my legs. Finley is jumping up and down."Thanks for fetching him dad."

"Don't even mention it kiddo. Anytime you need us we're there, you know that." He has a cup of tea waiting for me so we have a little chat at my kitchen table."If you can't talk to your mum, you know you can always come to me, don't you?"

I look up to my dad and wish I could crawl up into his arms. He may not realize it, but his words just made my insides crack a little. Talking to my dad is a lot different than talking with my mum. "I'm okay dad."

He doesn't buy it. "Kendal, your mum told me everything. I know she can be a pain but she's your mum, she cares for you. If you cannot talk to your mum, you always have me." I stand and rush into his big strong arms and snuggle into him. This is what I need, my dad. He squeezes me tight and kisses my forehead. "You're not on your own, got it?"

I nod because if I speak I will cry. I'm relieved he has not put the name Jax mum told him about to my Jax.

When my dad leaves I get out of my work clothes and pack me and Finley a sandwich and we're ready for the park.

Finley doesn't stop talking during the fifteen minute walk. He talks about his friends, what he did at school, Sam and Jessica's puppy, and he even shares his thoughts on my hair color.

We reach the park, and I sit on a bench watching Finley run like crazy. As I watch him, I think about telling Jax he has a son. I don't even know how to contact him, but I could bump into him or the band anytime soon. I now know it's best I tell him.

I need to properly think about how I'm going to do this. Jax tours the world now, and God knows what a rock star does. He might not even have the time for Finley. I look at my little boy and smile to myself. I can't believe how much he looks like his dad.

Chapter 9

Jax

I groan as I see at what I look like in the mirror and as soon as I make a sound, the curtains to my dressing room open. Rhys has a particularly smug smile on his face, looking pleased with himself. What a dick!

"Can't I just wear black jeans instead?"

"Nope, I say suits. It's my wedding, so what I say goes."

Leo and Max walk out of their changing rooms with the same look on their faces.

"Well, don't you guys look great."

Rhys is my best friend, but he better be careful right now. His smugness might get him a punch in the face. "Whatever."

Max shrugs his shoulders in his suit jacket, not looking very comfortable at all. Leo is pulling on the tie at his throat. They both have the black shoes on that Rhys picked out for us. I look down on the floor where mine are waiting for me. "I'm not wearing these shoes Rhys. I'll wear the suit for you, but not the shoes."

Leo walks over to stand by me and pats my shoulder. "I'm with Jax man, I hate these things. Please don't make me wear these."

Leo pouts and that almost makes me laugh, but I'm afraid if I do Rhys will make us wear the damn ugly shoes. Rhys looks over to Max who has turned to look at his reflection. That fucking vain bastard! "What about you, Max?"

"As much as I look like a good looking bastard right now, I'm with Jax. No to the shoes and I don't like these trousers either." He pulls on the waist of the trousers and frowns.

"No, you're all wearing the suits. I'm with you on these shoes though. We can all wear black Converse instead."

Thank fuck for that. I shove Rhys away, the little shit. I bet he knew all along we weren't wearing the shoes.

***

Today, the band has to attend some red carpet shit. It's for a movie premiere and I don't want to go. I hate these things and Rhys isn't that much of a huge fan of them either. I don't mind signing shit for the fans, that's part of being in a band; our fans are what make us. It's the stopping for pictures and interviews for the press that does it for me.

So the plan is we all do the red carpet, but Rhys and I aren't watching the film. We will leave after the red carpet and let Leo and Max stay for the after party. They love all the after party shit.

Times passes by without me realizing it. I hear the door bang open loudly. Laughter fills the house and I know what is about to happen even before I hear Leo shout. "PARTY TIME YOU SEXY MOTHER FUCKERS!"

The thumping sound of loud music fills the silence. I need to find my own place because these two have women around here all the time.

I decide to sneak out, so I quietly exit the game room. I don't know why because the music is so loud I can't hear any sounds I'm making and I'm sure nobody else will either. I open a door near my room that leads to a narrow staircase into the private living room. This room has a direct route to the garage, so I can get into my car without anyone from the party seeing me. I lock my bedroom door and I'm just about to open the door that leads to the stairway when arms wrap around my waist. A warm little body presses against my back. A sickly sweet smell fills my nose, and I pray to God it's not who I think it is.

"Hey, handsome."

Yep, it's Naomi. Why did the guys let Naomi in the fucking house?!

"What are you doing here, Naomi?"

I pry her arms from around me and turn to look at her. Her long blonde hair is falling down her back and her dull eyes are staring right at me, not hiding her lust."Why don't we go someplace private?"

Ugh, it makes me sick thinking of what we've done together. What did I ever think I would find with Naomi? Fuck all is what I got. "No can do, got someone to see."

"But I haven't seen you for ages. I came here to see you Jax."

Naomi did not take our breakup well. Being in a relationship with me brought her fame and attention. She started to get more modeling bookings, therefore making more money. She liked having the attention more than having a relationship.

"Another time maybe, I'm out."

I have no intention to spend any other time with her, but I need to get out of here. I feel her hand grip my arm.

"You don't want stay and have some fun? Like old times?" She places her hands on my chest.

"No thanks."

I quickly open the door to the stairway and disappear. I get into the DB9 and and head over to see Rhys. I definitely need to move the fuck out of that house.

Kendal

When I woke this morning I had a text on my phone waiting from Harley. He said he thought I looked gorgeous when he saw me and wanted to know if I was still able to catch dinner with him sometime. I didn't know what to say back so I ignored it.

I'm running a little late so when I enter Sophie's house I'm not surprised to see everyone here, they're all at the door and shout 'finally' in unison.

I'm handed a black dress bag with my name written in pink italic, nice touch. Then Sarah hands us a white shoe box each, the shoes! When we all open the boxes, all four of us gasp out loud. The heels are gorgeous and are full of sparkles that match the dresses completely. Sarah and Sophie stand at the other end of the room, facing away from us, waiting for the four bridesmaids to tell them when to turn around.

When we're all dressed we look at each other in awe. Wow! Sophie was right in mixing these dresses together, they look amazing. I look down at the shoes and they are perfect for the dress. The heels make the girls' legs look killer.

When Sophie turns around her eyes go all wide and shiny. She quickly wipes under her right eye and smiles at us all. "Wow girls, you all look so beautiful."

Her voice breaks a little, and we all rush over to her and hold her tight in a group huddle.

We admire ourselves in the mirror and talk excitedly about the wedding. The sparkling shoes bring out the sparkles on the dress even more. The cleavage on the boob tube corset is a heart shape on the cleavage which suits us all well. Once we are all back in our boring, normal clothes, Sarah says her goodbyes and we all head to the kitchen for a quick drink. Sophie shocks us and asks Tanya and I if we will take care of everything on the hair and beauty side for her big day!

Me and Tanya look to each other and grin. We both rush over to Sophie and squeeze her tight.

"Is that a yes?"

"YES!" We both shout. Sophie looks to me and asks if I will take care of her hair. I'm stunned, I thought she would want a big named professional for her bridal hair.

"Me?" My voice comes out a little squeaky and high-pitched. Sophie nods at me and holds my hands in hers.

"If I didn't meet you, I wouldn't have met any of you. You four girls mean a lot to me. I wouldn't want anyone else."

Sophie's has brought tears to my eyes. Of course, we're all involved now. Maisy is helping out with the house and garden transformation,

Jessica with the wedding cake and now Tanya and I are on the beauty side.

Chapter 10

This morning I was already awake when Finley came running in, so I surprise him. Before he has chance to shout me when he jumps on my bed I shout 'bo!' and he falls onto the bed laughing. I'm mostly laughing at Finley's deep chuckle. He sounds so adorable.

Finley's lying on his back, so I roll over and pin his arms down, he stops laughing and opens his eyes. He knows what I'm about to do. "Noooooo mummy! No tickles."

I see a little bit of his tummy peeking out from under his pajama top. His tummy sucks in as he takes a deep breath, waiting for me to do it. I suck in a deep breath and blow a long tickling raspberry on his little, soft belly. Finley bursts out a squealing laugh, and wriggles about on the bed. "Stop mummmmmy!"

I stop and lie back down, and Finley cuddles up to my side. "You're funny mummy."

I kiss him on his forehead, fighting that guilty feeling that is creeping back up. Finley has not demanded anything yet, so I quickly take advantage and get dressed. He doesn't give me time to do my hair though. "Juice mummy please."

I set about our morning routine. When we have both done in the kitchen, I take Finley back upstairs to get him dressed and tell him that we're going shopping.

On our drive into the town center, we sing along to the radio. One Direction comes on, and Finley knows almost every word. He's nodding his head as he sings and he belts out the last line. "That's what makes you beautiful!"

"Wow Fin that was great."

"I like singing. I'm gonna be the best singer ever mummy."

My heart stutters. He's only three, no need to panic. It would only be natural to follow in his dad's footsteps, even if he doesn't know Jax. I swallow down the ache in my heart. "Anything you want to be, rock star."

After we have been clothes shopping for a while we head up to the toy store. While he's browsing the toy shelves something catches my eye. I just grab it and ask the young girl behind the counter to hurry so my son cannot see me buying him a surprise. Once my secret purchase is hidden, I see Finley is looking at something. He looks like he's in deep thought. I step around the counter to see what he's looking at, and the ache in my heart returns in full speed that I almost fall to the floor. They're just toys, but I cannot help the thumping of my heart when I see the electric blue mic stand with microphone and the matching electric blue guitar. He doesn't know which one he wants more but I decide to spoil him and buy him both. He has a huge smile on his face while I'm struggling with the bags on the way to the car.

As soon as we get home he wants his new toys. He picks up the guitar and fits the sling over his shoulder and then stands behind his mic stand and starts shouting/singing."Oh yeah, I'm a rock star, rock star. I am a cool dude and my mummy has purple hairrrrrr!"

I can't stop laughing. That was the funniest thing I've seen in a long time. I wish I had recorded that."Wait, let me get a picture."

He acts like he's strumming his guitar and pulls a face. I snap away and send it to Jessica.

Jax

I'm in the garden with Max and Leo chilling by the pool with a few beers. We're sitting out here discussing the stag for Rhys. It's a little last minute, but we're guys and all we want to do is drink, so it is not going to be too much trouble. The guys want to have three days worth of strippers, but I say no, Rhys won't want that. We're using Leo's step brother's private plane because his step brother is a stinking rich film director.

Rhys loved Las Vegas when we toured there last year, but when you're on tour, you do not get to relax or see the sites. This time he will because that's where we are taking him. Max is looking for private villa's on his iPad when Leo claps his hands."We have to go to a strip club. We can have a private area just for us."

"When we were there last year Rhys said he wanted to go to the casinos but we didn't have time to."

Leo clicks his fingers. I look over to Max who has is busy booking shit."Yes, we should definitely do some gambling! Jax, you get on that."

Max looks up and frowns at Leo."And what is it you're gonna be doing?"

"Well, I got us the plane and thought of strippers. I've got a hot girl to see."

When the front door shuts behind him, Max shakes his head."Little shit always fucks off when stuff needs to be done."

Together Max and I manage to finish plans for Rhys.

Later on, I arrive at Rhys'. "Hey man, what are you doing?"

"What? Other than planning your stag?"

He grimaces. It's funny how scared looks."Oh shit."

I laugh and pat him on his shoulder as I walk past him and into his house. We walk into his huge garden."You need to get away from the guys again?"

"Yeah, but that's not why I'm here. I need to get a start on writing and your garden seemed the right place."

He leaves me to write because he knows I'm not good company when my mind is in another place. I zone out when I'm in my writing mode. If I get interrupted too many times, I snap and get in a bad mood. Too many times I've ended up in a fight or two with them over the years.

An hour and a half later, I feel like I've done enough. I have enough written down for about three songs. Rhys appears with a couple of beers and passes me one on his way to the seat across from me. "Is it safe to come out now?"

I laugh at the cheeky fucker.

"Good. I need to tell you something."

"Why didn't you tell me when I got here?"

He rolls his eyes at me like it is so obvious."You wanted to write, so I left you to it. You were all moody looking. It's one of your signs."

I laugh again and flip him the finger. "Say what you gotta say."

"I went for my usual jog the other morning and I saw James. It was about 5am, looked like he was doing the walk of shame."

My smile has now gone, and I take my own gulp from my beer. "Did you talk?"

What I wanted to say was, did he say anything about Kendal? Rhys shakes his head. "We both noticed each other and carried on. It was only at the bottom of the estate."

That close? If he was walking back to his place he must be close. Is Kendal close by too?

"I know what you're thinking, so stop it."

"What are you talking about?"

He raises his eyebrows at me."I've known you since we were fourteen, so I think I know how your mind works. Let me guess, you thought, does that mean Kendal is close by as well? Don't lie, I can tell by your face. You need to try and move on pal. It's been nearly four years since she walked away from you. She's a gorgeous girl. She's probably been snatched up by now and got herself a little family. You need to do the same. Don't get me wrong, I loved the girl, but I know how it has been for you since she left."

The thought of that devastates me. I know he's trying to make me realize I need to forget her, but the image of her married and happy with kids of her own hurt like hell. I know I still love her, and I can't help it. The thought of her with another man kissing him and letting him hold her angers me. She's still mine. I don't give a shit. I will see her, and I will win her back. I can't live like this anymore. I need Kendal back.

Chapter 11

Kendal

Tanya and I are rushing in our cars to Sophie's final dress fitting straight from work. With five minutes to go, we both snag side by side spaces in the car park down the road from the dress shop. We run towards the dressmaker's.

When we reach it we see it's not a dressmakers at all. It's a freaking posh up market wedding boutique. These places make me feel like shit.

I cautiously follow Tanya and we're greeted by a lovely elderly woman. She's all bright smiles and giggles. I feel a little more settled, but my surroundings are intimidating. The shop is filled with amazing beautiful dresses. Glass cabinets showing bridal jewelry. I don't go near those because I'm scared they will break if I go anywhere near them.

Tanya tells the kind lady we're here for Sophie James, and she happily shows us the way. This place is large. The front is where dresses and accessories are on show, and from there we walk further into the building. At the end, we reach a set of white double doors. She knocks on them and walks off. Where is she fucking going? One of the white doors is yanked open, and a young woman looks down her nose at Tanya and me straight away. This is the reason why I don't like these shops.

When we enter it becomes clear Sophie is a high paying customer because this is not your usual dressing room. I'm used to a little cubicle when I'm trying something new on. The bridal dressing rooms we just passed are what I expected from today. But this!

This room is huge. The girls are sitting on one of three golden leather sofas on the right hand side of the room. They're facing the middle where there's a golden platform that is raised slightly from the white wooden flooring. On the left side of the room, the whole wall is a mirror and right in front of me, facing the doors where we just entered, is a big area that is closed off by a golden curtain.

We're handed a glass of champagne by the woman who looked down he nose at me, as Sophie practically skips over to try on her dress.

We're all quiet, nobody talking because we're all anxious and excited to see Sophie. When the curtain moves, we all freeze in our seats and hold our breath. Out walks Sophie who has a beaming smile lighting up all her face. It looks like Sophie is floating across the floor to the platform. She stands facing the mirror and I cannot believe how amazing she looks, she looks absolutely beautiful. I suddenly feel so emotional. I can see Jessica wiping under her eyes in the reflection of the mirror. I knew she would be the first.

"So girls, do you like it?"

Sophie shifts her body side to side so the dress swishes around. It is an ivory color. The top is a halter neck style and shows a little cleavage. It looks like it is a smooth satin material and there are sparkling gems spotted around the bodice and halter neckpiece. The bottom puffs out, but not too much that she would not fit through the door. It's the same material as the halter neck top and doesn't have a lot of sparkle on it, but it looks perfect. Any more and it would be too much. She has on the same sparkly shoes as ours, which are just peeking out the bottom of her dress. None of us answer. I don't think we can. We look at each other and we all have shiny, teary eyes. Sophie turns around to face us and as soon as she takes a look at our faces she steps down off the little platform with her arms open wide.

"Oh you guys, come here."

We all put our glasses down, and rush over into a crying group hug. We're careful not to get any tears on the dress. After we have all got control over our emotions and wiped ours tears away on the soft tissues,we are all safe to talk again. Maisy is the first. "You look hot! Reece is not gonna know what to do when he sees you."

Tanya nods in agreement. "Yeah, your tits look amazing Soph."

"Oh girls I have some bad news. The guys have arranged Reece's stag for when we were supposed to be having the meal."

Oh that's a shame, I'm dying to meet him and finally see these friends of his. We all assure her that it's fine, we can still have the meal. After all, I'm going to bring Finley so Sophie can meet him before the wedding.

***

A couple of days later I wake up feeling like crap. I'm all sticky and sweaty and my stomach does not feel too good. I wish I could stay home in bed, but I have work. When Finley jumps on the bed, it makes my stomach feel worse. I hold the sickly feeling back and slowly get out of bed.

When I slowly walk into work, I go straight to the staff room. When I walk in, Tanya and Bianca are already there. After my first haircut of the day Bianca decides to send me home. Finley's at my mums so I go home and text her to say I'm at home sick. My mum comes by to bring Finley back later on and she puts him to bed for me. As soon as she is gone I fall into my bed and gladly fall asleep.

When my eyes open again, the sun is shining and Finley is sitting on my bed beside me. I smile up at him."My tummy feels sick mummy."

Oh no, now my little boy has what I had yesterday. I get us set up in my bed with one of Finley's DVDs and it's not long until he falls back to sleep next to me. Finley and I are supposed to be going to Sophie's for a meal. Finley's definitely not going, and I'm not leaving him. I decide to ring Sophie and explain why we won't be coming. She obviously understands and I spend the rest of the day cuddled with Finley in bed watching TV.

When Finley goes back to sleep I get out my iPad and plug in my headphones. I search for Jax Parker and listen to his interviews and watch some music videos. I even watch the interviews with Leo, Max and Rhys. I do miss those guys. Then I return to watching Jax and I cannot help but feel a need to be held by him. I miss him so fucking much it hurts.

Chapter 12

Jax

I laugh at the worried look on Rhys face when we're on the private plane. He glares over at me. "I'm glad you think this is so funny."

"Your face looks fucking hilarious."

Leo hands him a drink. "Drink up buddy! Soon we're going to be landing in Las Vegas baby!"

Rhys face is a picture. He looks at Leo, Max, his brother Rex, and then me. "Holy shit guys! This is gonna be fucking awesome!"

He starts chugging back his beer and we all follow. The stag do has started.

A private car takes us to the villa. It's a luxury pad with a pool and comes with a chef! Once we have dropped our bags off it's time to go to the casino. We all jump back into the limo and get ready to enjoy a night of gambling and drinking.

***

BANG BANG BANG

Someone please fucking make the banging stop! I'm lying face down on my bed. My legs are stiff from sleeping in my jeans. I guess that is better than waking up naked next to a girl I don't know. I'm trying to think back to last night, we spent most of the afternoon in the casinos and when we had enough, Leo and Max had arranged the limo to take us to a bar. We were the only guys there with about twenty of the most beautiful and sexiest women you will see dancing around waiting for us. Cheeky fuckers didn't tell me about that.

After so many drinks, I took notice to one of the girls, I can't remember her name. Her hair was dyed fire red, and she had shocking blue eyes, she was small and cute with big tits. We danced and did a few body shots, ended up kissing and I could have easily taken her back to our villa but something stopped me and I'm glad. I would have been pissed this morning.

BANG BANG BANG

"Jax, get up ya lazy shit!"

I smell bacon and sausages. I hear banging again but it's not my door this time."Bang again and I will fuck you up!"

I try to slowly get up, ignoring the dizziness. I find some fresh clothes and walk towards the bathroom. Ah fuck! Rex is sitting on the bathroom floor with his head on the closed toilet seat asleep. After I've finally managed to get a shower and had breakfast, made by Max and Leo while their dates for the night kiss them their goodbyes we leave for the activity day we hired out for today.

When we pull up in the limo all you can smell is petrol. Rhys jumps out the limo and stands beside me clapping my shoulder as he stands near."I can't fucking wait to get in one of those!"

After the boring safety talks we're off. Even though we were all hung over it was fucking awesome. Good job I hired it out all day because we kept going back for another race. I didn't join in when they went over to the bungee jump area. No fucking way, so Rex and I happily watched, laughing at their screaming.

We go back to our villa to change out of our dusty clothes. Max throws his arm around Rhys' shoulders. "Tonight we are getting bladdered. We're going home tomorrow, so we're making tonight count!"

Leo raises his hands in the air and shouts. "Let's get in that limo and get pissed!"

We pull up behind the strip club so nobody can get a picture of the groom-to-be coming in here. When I follow Rhys and step in the building my first thought is 'this place is fucking crazy.' No wonder the look on Rhys' face is slightly worried. This does not look like the usual strip joint. There are dancing girls naked in big cages dangling from the ceiling, there are two bars where dancing girls are performing, and there's three stages with two poles on each where girls are doing different shows.

A very attractive slim blonde girl approaches us. She is wearing hardly anything at all. She has a small red leather crop top on so we can all admire her flat stomach, and black shiny shorts that look more like underwear than shorts. We can see the bottom of her round bum cheeks. "I'm Britney. If you come with me, I'll show you to your private area."

She gives us all a smile and turns around. We all admire her firm arse peeking out under her shorts as we follow. Britney walks to one end of the club and up a set of stairs, I try not to stare too much at the view, but I see Max and Leo have no trouble. They're practically drooling. When we get to the top, Britney opens the nearest door and enters. The private room is huge. There's a sitting area with three tables and black leather sofas. At the far end of the room, is a stage with two dancing poles complete with two pretty girls.

"Right guys, this is your area for tonight. This is Tracy and Zara, your dancers. Some more girls will be with you later on in the night. Now let me take your drink orders."

Two girls walk in and serve us our drinks in gold bikinis. More girls join our room, giving us a girl-on-girl display dance. A cute little brunette starts to dance with her little bottom grinding on my lap. Max looks more interested in having an excuse to get Britney back up here to pay attention to his lap dance. Rex and Rhys are just enjoying watching after politely telling the girls they do not want a lap dance. Pussy whipped much?

At 3:00am Rex and Rhys decide to leave, I decide to leave with them. Leo and Max stay and have all the girls to themselves.

The next morning we all got up in the afternoon and went straight onto the plane for a nice quiet journey home.

Chapter 13

Kendal

Tomorrow I leave for Sophie's hen trip but I'm so sad to leave Finley. My mum is trying to cheer me up because I'm at my parent's to drop Finley off before I leave.

"Honey, just have fun. You deserve a girl's holiday, so you better enjoy yourself."

"I just feel guilty for leaving him. I'm going to miss him so much."

My mum rubs my back soothingly as we both stand at the back door watching Finley and my dad running around."Why? You never have time away. You deserve this. Two nights away is nothing."

Before I change my mind, I kiss and hug my parents goodbye. They give me their own little advice whilst hugging me.

"Stay away from those creeps Kendal. Keep safe. No sex and don't go anywhere on your own" Thanks a lot dad, how old am I again? He couldn't even look me in the face after he said the word sex. Where as my mum was the opposite as always,

"Enjoy yourself, show them what us real English women are like. Use protection baby." I don't know whose advice was worse. My dad must have heard my mum's because I saw him giving her an angry glare from across the room.

I tried not to squeeze Finley too much when I held him. "I'm going to miss you so much."

"I miss you mummy."

Oh no, do not cry, do not cry. I hug him tight and keep kissing his sweet little face and my heart melts at the sound of his laughing. I could feel my tears coming so I quickly say bye and run into my car where the tears freely fall.

At 7:00 the next morning I was at Jessica's house waiting for the white Hummer collect us, the rest of the girls were already inside, smiling and practically bouncing in their seats. Sophie was gobsmacked when she saw the plane. Sophie gave us a quick tour, there was even a bedroom at the back and Tanya couldn't help herself."So have you and Reece joined the mile high club up here Soph?"

Sophie actually blushed. The little tart!"I'm not telling."

She turns and goes to sit on one of the sofas and clicks her seat belt in place. Tanya goes to sit on the sofa opposite and does the same. "Oh my god, you totally have! Lucky bitch."

Our giggling gets cut off by the arrival of a very sexy male duo, who are decked out in uniform. They introduce themselves as the pilot and co pilot, and that we must take our seats as we're due to take off soon.

"I cannot believe you guys arranged this! I had no idea!"

"Well yeah, that was the idea."

Sophie playfully smacks Jessica on her arm and laughs. The flight attendant serves us champagne. I recline my chair and start to relax, my eyes feel a little heavy but Maisy jolts me awake. "Can we tell her now please?"

We all agreed that when we told her, we would count down on the plane. This is the right time I suppose. "Three! Two! One! Barcelona!"

Sophie gasps and covers her mouth with her free hand."Oh my god guys!"

When we land we're a little tipsy already. We all sigh in appreciation for the heat when we step out the plane. There's a limo already waiting for us. When the limo takes us to the hotel, we all stare wide eyed at each other. Surely this is not where we are staying? It's so glamorous. Not at all the type of hotel I would normally book, because I wouldn't be able to afford it. Maisy had got in contact with Reece for the details of the private plane that his friend hired to us for free! Hearing what we were up to for his future wife, he wanted to take care of the right hotel for Sophie and we agreed. I know for a fact that Reece paid for most of this and only took a tiny amount from us all to humor us.

We get escorted to our room, which is breathtaking. Sophie gets the main bedroom which has a huge queen sized bed, seeing as she is the bride. Jessica and I share the second room which has double beds in it, and Maisy and Tanya share the last room which is identical to mine and Jessica's.

"Erm guys I don't know what to change into. What are you all wearing?" Sophie comes into our room and is looking nervous. She has no idea where we are going or what we have planned.

"Wear a bathing suit or bikini with something over it so you're not walking around in it."

When we are all ready we are driven to Sophie's surprise. When we pull up at the row of small boats and yachts, Sophie is the first one out the car. "Oh my god, no way!"

We walk along the boats all bobbing in the water until we reach ours. We found a company who deals with hen and stags for overseas it was pretty easy to choose what to do. We see the woman who we are supposed to meet standing beside a slick sexy white yacht. There's a minibar on board with a sitting area and then a big area up front where we can all lay and sun bathe. Music is playing for us, and it is not long until we're beyond tipsy and laughing way too much. It's a good girly way to spend the day. Out on the sea, getting a tan with a glass of bubbly. We take so many photos and ask the woman, who's name is Cathy, to take some group photos for us.

After an amazing afternoon, we're back on land. Sophie cannot stop thanking us."Oh my guys, I cannot believe you arranged that! It was so much fun, the music, sun, champagne and the freaking yacht!"

"Glad you enjoyed it babe."

Maisy grabs her into a drunken embrace, and we all follow as we make our way back to the waiting limo. We decide to get changed into sexy dresses for our meal before we explore the nightlife.

***

The next morning my head is so sore. We didn't get in until 3:00am. I never usually get that drunk. We ended up joining a bar crawl and the organizer made us do a whole lot of drinking games. I feel a body shift next to me and freeze. Oh shit! I didn't bring anyone back, did I? I think back to all the guys we danced with, and what we were up to but I can't remember coming back with a guy. Fucking hell, have I had sex with someone and not remembered anything?

"Relax it's me you fart."

My eyes snap open and I see Jessica lying next to me smiling. She looks a right mess, hair all over her pillow, yesterday's make-up all over her face. "Looking very attractive this morning."

I must be the same mess as her then. I smell the alcohol on her breath and cringe. "Neither is your breath."

She shoves me hard but I'm still half asleep and hung over so I fall off the bed. Fucking bitch! I can hear her laughing. I slowly pick my sore body from off the floor, now I'm standing I see I'm in a different room. Why am I in Sophie's room? Then I see Sophie peek out from under the quilt on the other end. "Argh it's too bright."

We all freshen up and wash away the dirt sweat and make-up from yesterday and are all in the living area relaxing and talking over last night, filling in each other gaps what we can't remember. We order room service because we can't be bothered to go down to the dining rooms downstairs in the hotel.

After breakfast, we all decide to go down to the pool. I'm watching the girls in the pool and Sophie laughs on the sun lounger next to me. "Oh God, Kendal come here."

I look across to her and inwardly cringe. She has her camera out. I can only guess what pictures were snapped last night. I looked at mine this morning. There are some shockers on there. I drag myself up, and Sophie shows me what has made her laugh. There on the little screen on her camera is a picture of me bent over in front of Tanya in a doggy style position but that's not all. Sophie is standing in front of me holding a hot dog sausage like she has a dick and the end is in my mouth. So I'm in a threesome with Sophie and Tanya.

"Ohhhhh my God!" Jessica appears behind us and peers over our shoulders. She is bent over laughing.

"Yeah keep laughing, wait until you see mine Jess." She stops laughing and comes to sit by me, probably worrying what dirty picture I snapped of her. She should be worried. I reach for my camera and turn it on and search through my pictures. When I find it Jessica stares at the picture wide eyed and her mouth hanging open. It's a picture of Tanya and Jessica, both on stripper poles. Sophie and I cannot hold back our laughter while Jessica sits back in embarrassment.

After another half an hour we decide it's time to get ready for today. When we're back in our room, we tell Sophie to get changed into something cool and comfortable. Tanya is very excited for today, I am actually, it should be a laugh.

"We're gonna get all sweaty today!" Tanya is singing from her room and I see Sophie thinking over what we could be doing. I hope she likes it. She didn't like sex shops so I hope having pole and lap dancing lesson will be okay. If anything, she can show Reece everything she has learned. I'm sure he will thank us, especially when they get the dancing pole Tanya picked up for a wedding present. A couple more photos and we make our way down to the limo.

Sophie's face was priceless when we told her what was happening. It was so much fun and I was right in thinking we would have a laugh. Pole dancing is hard work, no wonder there are no fat strippers. We learned some cool tricks by the nice instructors and when they taught us some moves we put them to a dance, it was amazing. After an hour, we moved on to the lap dance lesson. We were grinding on the lap of an invisible man to begin with. The next step is to give an actual man a lap dance. Right on cue, five stupidly sexy men walk in. We all looked to each other, holy fuck!

The guys were all tan with dark hair. Their bodies were muscled and trim. I couldn't stop staring. The instructors introduced us to them as they paired us off. The hunk of male I was paired with was named Miguel. He had muscles everywhere on his golden skin.I felt extremely awkward but powerful whilst performing my little lap dance on Miguel. I knew that my cheeks were blushed by the burning I felt. He had a sexy grin on his face as I kept turning to look at him, at the part of the dance where we drop low and hold our bottoms in the air I caught him staring at my behind with heat in his eyes. Oh wow, what those eyes did to my girly parts.

I was glad when it was finished to be honest, the hen planning website said nothing about this part of the lesson! When we had finished, the girls were chatting and gathering out stuff when Miguel approached me. He wanted to know how long we were staying for and if we're going out tonight. I told him the truth, we're going tomorrow and yes we're going out but when he asked if I wanted to meet tonight I declined. I am not one of those girls, I don't like one night stands. On our drive back, Tanya is in her element. "Holy shit those guys were hot."

At 9:00pm we all have our mini dresses and heels on, all of us are looking sexy as hell if I do say so myself. We ask the young man on the reception to take pictures of us before we leave. He could not disguise his wide eyes and blushing.

It was now early morning and we were all extremely tipsy. It wouldn't be too long until we were going back to the hotel. Just our luck as we're at the bar some very attractive men approach us and I realize it is Miguel, Andre and their friends. They offer to buy us drinks, and I can feel Miguel's eyes on me all the time. I look up at him as I sip from my drink. He winks at me and steps closer. Tanya walks off with Andre, her dance God. Maisy walks with them talking to a friend of Andre's. Sophie and Jessica walk away so now I'm on my own with the very sexy Miguel. Thanks guys!

Miguel gently places his big hand on my shoulder and steps closer, so close were nearly touching. "You look very beautiful in that dress."

I can feel my cheeks heating. Tonight I'm wearing my red peplum dress paired with my five inch wedge heels. My dress fits tight across my chest making my C cups look a size bigger. It smoothly skims over my plump backside and is very short, which I'm thinking is why he thinks I look beautiful. I would be annoyed, but that damn sexy accent sways me. I smile at him. "Thank you, you don't look too bad yourself."

He chuckles deep in his throat. We talk for about five minutes and then when I've finished my drink, he whisks me off to the dance floor.

Miguel can dance! His hands trail all over me, his mouth comes so close to my skin I can actually feel his lips. His body moves against mine so sinfully it's like he is giving me a little preview to how sex with him would be. I'm thinking it would be pretty amazing going by this dance. I glance over at Sophie and Maisy who are dancing together happily. They both see me looking and give me a thumbs up. I feel as though they're giving me the approval to sleep with him, but I don't know if that's a good idea. Tanya and Maisy very passionately kiss Miguel's friends and I feel Miguel pull me closer. He turns me so my back is pressed onto his front, his hands wrap around my front. His head nudges mine to the side a little and he runs his mouth up and down my throat, his stubble scratches my skin and sends shivers along my body.

He whispers tempting words into my ear and I fill with desire. I haven't had sex for a year! lean my head back on his shoulder but he turns me quickly, so I'm facing him again. His hands drift down and squeeze my bottom."How about we carry that tempting dance of yours to mine?"

I freeze. Do I really want to? I feel like I do, but logic has me second guessing.I bite my lip and see Miguel staring at my lips. Why am I thinking through this so bad? I have never done this before, I am twenty-four and I have never had a one night stand. I have slept with two men, and that is because I was in a relationship with them. I have an unbelievably sexy hunk of a man with me who is asking if I want to spend the night with him. He's making me want sex by his dancing. I think I do want to go back with him.

I cannot believe I'm going to do this but fuck it, I'm going home tomorrow. When I look up to tell him yes, I can't do it. This is not me and it never will be. I've had sex with two men for Christ sake! I'm not one night stand type of girl. I like to know the guy, and I'm proud to say the two men I have had sex with I know and are great guys. It doesn't hurt that Harley and Jax are deliciously sexy, but that's not the point. No matter how sexy Miguel is, I can't spend tonight with him. "I can't, I'm sorry."

He slowly nods and shrugs his shoulders at me then walks away to his crowd of friends. I half laugh and half scoff. What a dickhead! I'm suddenly very happy I decided not to spend the night with him.I have a fabulous end of the night with my girls, apart from Tanya and Maisy who have already left. I noticed that Miguel left with them too.

***

I hear a banging on the door and wince. My head hurts. I manage to peel my eyes open and I notice that I'm not in my bed, I'm on the sofa in the living area."Will you lazy bitches get up and answer the damn door!"

I pull my body up and walk across the nice cold floor to the door. My eyes are still partly closed when I open the door for the one night standers. I leave them to close the door and go to my room so I can lie on my bed. I'm not allowed any more sleep, because the girls follow me in and sit on the edge of my bed, happily chatting away. They wake Jessica and Sophie, who are in the next bed. Jessica grabs a pillow and throws it at Tanya. It hits her straight in the head. "What was that for?"

"Shut up! We were sleeping!"

Sophie leans up on one elbow. "So what did you two get up to last night?"

Apparently Miguel paired up with Andre and gave Tanya a good old threesome.

When I come out all clean from my shower, wearing my short light blue denim shorts that are dip dyed pink and my white vest top. When we are all ready we walk to the beach which is just around the corner from our hotel. When we reach the beach, Sophie links our arms together and smiles up at me. She looks so happy and I feel proud that we, as her friends, played a part in that. "So what are we doing on the beach?"

"You will find out."

I spot the photographer further down the beach. When we reach her Sophie still seems a little confused.

"Hi girls. I'm Sophia. I will be taking your photos."

"Photos?" Sophie's face is scrunched up in thought, how could she have not pieced this together yet?

"We have arranged for some pictures to be taken of us on the beach, Soph."

The morning was spent having fun on the beach in front of the camera. There were shots of us eating ice cream, jumping around, splashing in the sea. We have some dinner and then head back to our hotel to pack before we go home. I am so excited to see Finley. I rang him every morning and every night before we went out but it is nothing compared to seeing his beautiful face.

On the plane home, Sophie stands up from the sofa and looks at each of us. "Right girls before we go home, I just want to say thank you. I knew you would do me proud and give me a great hen, but I never imagined this. Every minute has been amazing and I never even thought about Barcelona!"

She gives us all a hug and a kiss and she starts crying, so it turns into a bit crying group hug. "I just cannot believe I'm getting married in two days!"

We stop her crying and laugh over the memories from the last couple of days.

Chapter 14

I leave my suitcase near the washing machine. It's nice to be home. I look at my phone with longing, I want to see Finley but it's 7:30pm so he will probably be in bed now.

The house is way too quiet, so I put the TV on and catch up on my missed programs. Half way through the first, I feel my eyes getting heavy.

I wake up from the ringing of my phone. The living room is now dark, crap I fell asleep.

"Hello?" My voice sounds all croaky from sleep.

"Kendal? Were you asleep?"

"Yea, what's up?"

"Oh sorry. Look, I need to see you."

"What? Why?"

"Just get here Kendal, now."

The line goes dead. I cannot believe she hung up on me! Rather than be annoyed, I'm really worried. All the way to Sophie's, I'm praying that she is okay.

I buzz when I reach her gates and race up to her house. Something is definitely off. Sophie normally shouts her hello as I come in through the gates. I park my car, run to the front door, and knock. Sophie answers straight away and I know by her face something's up. She gives me a little smile, and moves to the side so I can walk in. I'm starting to get really worried now. So I walk into the hallway. I turn around to face her, and she closes the door and turns to me. "Soph?"

She suddenly looks up and walks over to me. She has tears in her eyes. "I can't believe it's you. He always spoke about you. I just can't believe

I found you for him."

"Sophie, what are you talking about?"

"I showed Reece the pictures from the hen and he recognised you. I didn't think it was you, I thought it was a different Kendal. Why didn't you tell me?"

Her little face looks hurt.

"Sophie what are you tal-"

"Hi Kendal."

At the sound of his voice, I stop talking and freeze. It could not be. I slowly look to my right and there standing before me is Rhys. He looks sad but he's smiling at me. I choke back a sob. I honestly just want to run into his arms, but I've not seen him for so long. For fuck's sake, why didn't I see the signs? Decoy moves back. I meet Sophie in the best hotel in town, and she tells me her boyfriend's name is Reece. I didn't know her Reece was actually Rhys! He steps closer. "As soon as Sophie showed me her pictures, I knew it was you Kenny."

Kenny was the nickname they all gave me. Hearing him call me that brings tears to my eyes. This is so fucked up and confusing. I cannot do this right now. With my eyes closed to stop my tears, I don't see him quickly come closer and wrap me in his arms. He squeezes me tight and I try my hardest to fight back my sobs. When he kisses me on my hair and then on my forehead, they fall on their own.

When I left Jax, I left the guys too and through the two years I was with Jax, Rhys, Leo, and Max became like my brothers. I left them too and didn't say goodbye. I've lied to them too. Not only has Finley been missing out on having Jax as his dad, he has missed out on having them as his uncles. I cry in Rhys' arms, and then break away. I need to go home. I need to get my head around this. I step towards the door and Rhys tries to reach me, but I move out of reach. "Kendal, please stay, Jax is on his way."

My eyes widen and stumble a little. They told Jax I was here? I cannot be here when he comes. He can be here any minute. I need to go. "I can't do this, I'm sorry."

I turn and run out of their house and yank open my car door. My hands are shaking as I get my keys. Rhys comes and stands by the car. I can hear what he's shouting but I'm choosing to ignore him. He thinks I shouldn't drive, that it's dangerous, but I need to go. My wheels screech as I pull away from the house and race back down their drive. I try to get my breathing in control as I drive home. As I'm driving, passing big houses alongside Sophie's, I see an extremely nice sports car approaching. I'm not particularly good with cars. As it comes side by side, I can make out who the driver is. It's dark but I know that person all too well and by the looks of it, Jax saw me too. Shit!

I try to drive faster down the road, and turn left so he cannot follow my car. I hear the screeching of tires and pray he has not seen where I've gone. I decide to drive home through the little streets along the other houses rather than the big open road because I can lose Jax that way.

Jax

I was bored shitless at home when Rhys rang me.*"I'm about to tell you something big, so don't freak out alright?"*

"Okaaayy."

I hear him breath heavily down the phone.*"Sophie just came back from her hen trip with her girlfriends. I asked to see some photos and guess what I saw?"*

"Some sexy girl on girl pics?"I would definitely love to see those.

"Erm no. The new friends she's been talking about. Well, shit, those girls are Jessica, Tanya, Maisy and Kendal."

I nearly drop the phone in shock. All along it has been Kendal, Jess, Tan and Maisy. Fucking hell, all along she has been right there.

"Jax?"

"Yeah I'm here."

"Kendal's on her way over."

"You sure this is my Kendal."

"She's changed her hair but yeah. It's Kenny alright."

I smile at hearing the nickname the guys gave her."And she's coming to yours?"

"I can see her getting out her car now."

"Why didn't you ring me sooner?"

I jump up and start to put some clean clothes on. If I'm seeing Kendal, I want her to see me at my best."*Sophie didn't think it was a good idea."*

When I was at my worst, before I met Naomi, I would talk to Sophie about the girl that I loved and had got away. She would talk to me about the girl she had never met, and it helped me get myself together. I couldn't talk to the guys about what I was going through. I hear Rhys inhale, I know he can see Kendal. I wish I was there so bad. "Woh."

"I'm on my way, make sure she stays."

As I'm speeding down the empty road in front of Rhys, I catch sight of a Beetle. I hate those fucking ugly cars, but as I'm looking at the car with disgust, I see the driver. Even though her hair's not the same bright red as it used to be, I would know that girl anywhere. I hit the brakes and spin as fast as I can. Good thing there are no other cars on the road. Once my car stopped spinning, I see her car turn left at the end of the road, so I quickly race after her. I know she's trying to lose me, but I will not let her get away this time. I reach the road she disappeared down and punch the steering wheel. I've fucking lost sight of her.

I drive around for a little while and listen out to see if I can hear another car. I can't find that ugly car anywhere. I turn around and drive back the way I came and pull up in front of Sophie and Rhys' house. Rhys opens the door before I knock, he says nothing, just moves to the side to let me in. We go and sit in their large living room.

"I didn't think it was her Jax. I had no clue." Sophie's voice is just above a whisper. I look at her and she's looking down at her hands.

"It's fine, Soph."

"I just can't believe it's her. You've told me everything about her and now I see it."

"Do you know where she lives?"

She bites her lip and shakes her head."I've never been to her house, but I've been to Jessica's and I know she lives around the corner."

I stand. I need to find her."Let's go then."

Sophie looks shocked."I can't do that Jax. I'm sorry. She's my friend too, I can't do that to her. I'll talk to her and ask."

She gets her phone and leaves the room. I sit back down and Rhys gives me a sad smile. We sit in silence for a couple of minutes.

"You're gonna cum in your pants when you see her on Saturday."

Saturday? Oh shit, the wedding! She's a bridesmaid. I can watch her all day, talk to her and maybe sneak a dance? I can't wait that long though. I need to see her before the wedding. Sophie walks in with tears in her eyes. "She's not answering my calls."

Rhys gets up and holds her. "She will be fine,. Kendal won't be upset with you. Try the girls."

She types away on her phone and then holds it to her ear.

"Jess?..... Have you heard from Kendal?..... I can't get hold of her......No he hasn't.....Is she okay?.......Can I come round?.......Okay then, I'll see you then, bye"

She sits down on a huff. "So?"

Rhys scowls at me.

"She's over at Sam and Jess's house. They're taking her home. Sam had her phone just in case you had her number, but I told her you haven't. All the girls are going over at 7:00 tomorrow night to have a drink."

"Why that late?"

"She has work all day and then she has Finley."

Sophie shrugs her shoulders like it is obvious. Finley? Is this her new boyfriend? Well, I will see to it that Kendal's mine and nobody else is having her.

"Is it okay if I stay here tonight?"

Sophie looks up to me and smiles. Her tears are now gone. "Of course, your rooms always ready for you."

"Thanks, I'm gonna up now. Could you let her know I want to see her tomorrow?"

She nods and looks away, Rhys gives me a head nod before I go to bed. I don't think I'll be able to sleep though.

Chapter 15

Kendal

Jessica and Sam took me home and I'm now on my own, lying in my bed. I don't know why I stopped in front of their house. I just sat in my car in complete shock. It took ten minutes for a worried Sam to guide me out the car. For a while, I couldn't say a word to them, I just sat there in total silence; ignoring them. When I realized I was worrying them I told them what had happened.

While lying on my bed, my phone suddenly rings, it makes me jump. It's Sophie calling again. I think about rejecting her call but then I've already missed three calls from her. Sophie was not to know about Jax and I."*Kendal, thank god, I've been so worried. Are you mad? I totally understand, I'm so sorry. I didn't know Rhys told Jax to come. I'm so sorry."*

I decide to stop Sophie's ranting. "Sophie, its fine. There's nothing to worry about, I'm just shocked, that's all."

"I can understand that. Look I don't want to say this, but Jax has asked if you will see him tomorrow. He wants to meet you before the wedding."

I can understand why he wants to meet me, but I'm still confused, it's still a lot to get my head around at the minute. I appreciate the fact that she hasn't told Jax where Jess and I live, because despite the fact that she knew Jax first, she still upholds our special sister bond. "*He still loves you Kendal. He talks about you all the time. He's never gotten over you; I love him like a brother so I feel a little protective of him. I know he wants you back, just don't break his heart again, please. I know you have this bond with Finley's dad, and then there's Harley."*

Jax has spoken to Sophie about me? He didn't forget about me? I feel guilty that Sophie doesn't know that Jax is Finley's dad. I think I will tell her tomorrow; just not over the phone."Are you coming with the girls tomorrow?"

"Of course, I will definitely be there. Will I finally get to meet the gorgeous Finley?"

"Yes, you can finally meet him and I might as well start on your nails for Saturday."

We say our goodbyes and I lay in bed waiting for sleep to finally overtake me.

* * *

The following morning, my alarm wakes me up at 7:00am; I jump up despite being exhausted. Today I'm going to see my gorgeous little boy! I'm so excited I feel like jumping around and screaming. I quickly get ready in to my work gear, black leggings and purple vest top, then shove my hair up in to a messy ponytail. I groan in frustration when I realize my car is still parked outside Jessica's. I arrive at my parents at 7:15. I walk straight into their house. All thoughts of last night are long forgotten right now. When I enter the first words I hear are Finley's.

"Mama Juice pleeease."

"Okay Finley."

"And biscuits."

I hear my dad laughing. "I thought you wanted cereal Fin?"

"Kay Grandad, Grandmama cereal too pleeease."

Oh my god, I've missed that so much. I quickly sneak past the stairs so Finley cannot see me, I sit at my parents kitchen table and wait. I hear them come downstairs, I'm practically bouncing in my chair. Finley is the first one to walk into the kitchen. His eyes quickly scan the kitchen and then jump back to me realizing that I'm sat here with a huge grin plastered on my face. I start to cry at the look on his face, I've missed my son so much!

"Mummy!" He screams at the top of his voice and runs towards me. I open my arms and wrap them tightly around him. I'm sobbing when he's cuddled in my arms. I've not seen him for four nights; I realize now that the time apart feels like I've not been breathing, without him I'm empty.

"Oh god Finley, I missed you so much."

"I miss you mummy."

I pull him back so I can look at his perfect little face. He has tears in his eyes and my heart breaks. "Oh honey, what's the matter?"

"I miss you mummy."

His voice breaks as he buries his face back into my neck and holds on tight to me. My heart just broke a little more. "Oh I missed you so much. You're sleeping in my bed tonight because I want to cuddle you all night."

He pulls away and wipes at his eyes. His face lights up in a big smile. "I like your bed."

"I know you do."

He sits on my knee while he eats his breakfast, not wanting to be away from me.

Chapter 16

I get to spend a couple of hours with Finley before the girls all come over. I don't really want Finley at the wedding now that I know Jax will be there. I know Jax should know about him and I am going to tell him but I think I should wait until after the wedding. I don't want drama to disturb Sophie's wedding. When I asked Finley if it was OK he stayed at my parents he seemed happy enough. He thought the idea of a wedding was disgusting and didn't want to see old people kiss.

As it gets closer to when the girls arrive I decide to send Sophie a text asking about Jax.

ME: What did Jax have in mind?

SOPHIE: Dinner? Or would u rather just meet and talk?

ME: Dinner, if that's OK? What time?

I don't get a message back for about fifteen minutes and it makes me feel slightly nauseous.

SOPHIE: He will pick you up at 9.30, wear a nice dress and heels, I have a feeling he's booked to impress u honey. I need ur address x

He's taking me somewhere to impress me? He doesn't need to impress me; I loved him before he had anything. I think about how I'm going to tell Sophie. She's going to see Finley tonight; as soon as she looks at him she is going to know.

At 6:00 there's a knock on the door, I know it is going to be Jessica so when I open the door I'm not surprised that I get swallowed by her tiny arms. "Oh Kendal how are you?"

"Fine."

"I've been worried all day."

"Jess, I'm fine."

She holds me back and narrows her eyes at me. "You're fine?"

"Yeah and I'm meeting Jax at 9:30."

Before she can say anything else Finley runs up to Jessica and we move into the living room. Not long after Jessica's arrival, Maisy is here shortly followed by Tanya who picked Sophie up on the way. When I see Sophie, I start to get nervous. I've already told the girls we need to tell Sophie.

Tanya walks straight in to my house, like she normally does. I see Sophie following behind her and she looks a little awkward so I grab her in a tight hug. I hear her sniff a few times; I know she's shed a few tears.I hear Finley laugh in the living room and Sophie looks in that direction, I know she's dying to meet him. I've denied her this for so long, so I take her by the hand and lead her into the living room, fighting down my sickly nerves I notice when we step into the living room Sophie's body goes stiff. Finley is in his pajamas and laughing at Jessica. I get Finley's attention, he walks over a little shyly."Finley this is my friend Sophie."

He looks to think for a minute and then he smiles his megawatt smile at Sophie. So much like Jax my heart squeezes."Hi Sophie."

"Hi Finley." Her voice sounds high pitched and croaky. Finley runs back to Maisy and Jessica and I look at Sophie. Her eyes are wide and have tears in them with her mouth is hanging open a little.

Yep, she knows. How could she not when he gave her the typical charming Jax smile? "Soph?"

She tears her eyes away from Finley and looks at me. "Kendal?"

I look over to Maisy and Jessica who have now both stood up. Maisy takes hold of Finley's hand and takes him out of the room, giving me a wink as she passes me.I lead Sophie onto the sofa, followed by Jessica and Tanya."When did you leave Jax?"

I swallow hard. Sophie is piecing it together. "Four years ago."

She nods."And how old is Finley?"

I clear my throat."He's four next month."

She nods her head and then slowly looks at me dead in the eye."How could you do that? This is what he has wanted all these years. He's been lost without you."

I hang my head in shame. I feel awful. This is making me feel like shit, I know it's only going to be worse when I finally tell Jax. I explain everything to Sophie, every feeling I have, my thoughts on why I did this and every memory that I can remember from when I first saw those two lines on the test that confirmed I was pregnant, and everything else that has happened right up until the present moment. I know that I have made a mistake, I do regret it but I still stand by my decision.

I don't think Jax would have reached his dream if I told him I was pregnant. When I've finished talking, everyone's quiet apart from Finley who is shouting and laughing from his bedroom upstairs. I no doubt have a messy face from my tears.I finally look at Sophie, scared at what I will see but what I see surprises me. She is looking at me with such pity in her eyes. Her face is wet with her tears and her hand is clutching her heart. "Oh my god Kendal, I'm so sorry!"

She wraps her arms around me, and when she does I cry in her arms. I hear Sophie crying too. When we have stopped and we're tear free, we smile at each other and Sophie smoothens my hair."Are you going to tell him tonight?"

"I was thinking I should meet him after your wedding to tell him. I don't want there to be an atmosphere on Saturday."

"OK, as much as I don't like it, I wont say anything. If you don't tell him by the time I'm back from my honeymoon though, I will tell him."

"I promise."

"He looks exactly like him, it's unreal."

We play and talk to Finley until it's time for him to go to bed. He pouts his sad face.

"Say night to the girls." He gives Jessica, Maisy, and Tanya a hug and a kiss goodnight and then he gets to Sophie. Finley wraps his little arms around her Sophie leans down to kiss his head. I can see tears in her eyes.

When Finley's asleep and the girls nails are all done it's time for me to get ready to see Jax.I look in my wardrobe, I don't know what to wear. I'm starting to freak out. I'm seeing Jax in about two hours! Instead of standing in my room in a panic I grab my make up and hair supplies and decide to get ready downstairs with my girls.

At 8:30 my make-up is looking flawless. Tanya is straightening my hair. "I cannot believe you're going to see him."

Jessica looks very excited for me."I'm so happy for you."

Tanya frowns at Maisy. "Why? She's a nervous wreck, she hasn't seen him for four years and she has his secret child. She's going to clear the air with him for Sophie's sake. Even if she does still love him "

Sophie gasps."You still love him?"

Well I thought that was obvious, wasn't it? I just nod instead; I don't know what to say. Sophie looks like she is going to cry. "Kendal this is so romantic! You can reunite. After all these years."

It can't be that simple, can it? I still love him. In a perfect world I would be back in Jax's arms, but he's probably a completely different person now. He's a huge famous rock star and I'm still me, plus I've kept a massive secret from him. It doesn't matter if he still loves me or not, the truth is, I'm going to hurt him when he finds out.

Tanya, my ever so protective friend when it comes to the topic of Jax, finishes my hair and steps in. "It's not that simple though, they have had a lot of time apart. Kendal's tried to move on and I bet Jax has."

"Well yes, but it hasn't worked out for either of them because they still love each other."

They're both speaking the truth but I have no idea what to say. I try anyway."Look, tonight is a meeting so there's no tension on Saturday. I will meet him after the wedding, I plan to tell him everything. I can only hope that he wont hate me too much and we can at least be friends for Finley's sake. In all honesty I'm not expecting anything, and I don't think

I should expect anything from him anyway."

Maisy and Sophie frown at me but Jessica and Tanya are nodding their agreement.Maisy and Sophie are the helpless romantics here. They just want me to fall back in Jax's arms and be a happy little family. Jessica and Tanya are the realists.They had always been the ones to fight my corner first with this subject; even though they were the ones who voiced their disagreement on my decisions more than what anyone else did, in the end they always supported me.

Maisy speaks up. "But if he forgave you and you still love him, why can't you be together?"

Jessica scoffs and replies. "Erm because he's some huge rock star now who goes everywhere and she would probably hardly ever see him."

Well shit why I did not think of that. I decide to speak for myself. "It's not just that. I've been trying to move on for four years, I didn't think I would see him again. After all of this time, it's going to be really strange seeing him. I can't just be with him straight away, no matter how much I want to. I need to get used to seeing him again first. Then there's Finley, all of a sudden he's going to go from not seeing Jax to then suddenly having him in his life. It will confuse him if suddenly Jax and I become a couple straight away, he has to get used to seeing his dad first."

Everyone is quiet for a few minutes.

"I'm sorry Kendal."

"I didn't think of that, sorry."

"Honey, it is going to be fine."

"We're here for you, always."

They all fuss over me, helping me finish to get ready.When my hair is looking silky straight, we all head to my room to look at my clothes to decide what I should wear.

Sophie has asked Jax where he's taking me tonight; he's told her that we are going to Eclipse! It's the most fanciest and expensive restaurant in town! I've never been there; it's where all the super rich people go. You have to look the part to get inside, I've heard that to get a table you have to book months in advance. So how the hell did he get a table at such short notice?

We look at my favourite dresses that are on my bed. "You need to look sexy."

Sophie nods at Tanya. "But also sophisticated"

Jessica holds up a black dress and shakes her head no.

They all choose a red dress that is molds my curves and makes my tits look amazing! Tanya throws it at me and demands that I put it on. I don't know if I'm brave enough to wear this tonight. When I have it on, I look in my full length mirror.   I smile at my reflection, I do look good, I look elegant and I feel sexy, but not in your face slutty sexy. The dress hugs my body like it is made for me. The girls all give me the thumbs up along with their huge smiles. Paired with my shiny nude colored five inch heels I'm ready to go.

It's 9:15 and I'm a nervous wreck. In fifteen minutes Jax will arrive at my house. Fucking hell!

Maisy places a big glass in front of me. I raise my eyebrows.

"A big glass of Vodka and Lemonade is what you need right now."

I thank her and start drinking. The girls try to help distract me from my nervousness, but I feel sick. Should I really be doing this? "Guys do you think I'm over dressed?"

They frown and all reply at the same time. "No!"

"You don't think I look too sexy do you?"

They all smile and again they all say the same thing at the same time; "Yes."

I get up to look at my dresses again when there's a knock at my front door. Oh shit. At the same time, I feel my phone vibrate.

Chapter 17

Jax

I can't believe my luck that Kendal wants to meet up with me tonight. I booked the best place in town, not only to impress Kendal but at Eclipse I can make sure we have a private table. We can talk undisturbed, which makes it well worth the money. When I booked the table, I informed the restaurant that I'm not the 'suit and tie' type of guy. Once I told them who I was, they assured me that they didn't care what I wore, they just wanted me there. They will probably tip the press for free publicity. I just hope they can keep quiet until after our meal.

When I pull up in front of Kendal's house, I realize how close I was to finding her last night. I feel like a nervous teenager on his first date. What's wrong with me? I know Kendal. I still love her, I haven't seen her yet, but I know I want her to be mine again. I hope tonight goes smoothly; I want to be on her good side, otherwise I will have no chance of getting her to love me again. Getting out of my car, I head to the front door, I knock and wait.

Rhys secretly gave me Sophie's camera last night, so that I could have a peek at the photos from Sophie's hen trip. I was blown away by how amazingly beautiful Kendal looks. She's so fucking gorgeous. But then I got pissed off at some of the other pictures; ones with her dancing with guys, then other images taken with other men, standing behind her drooling and leering over her. Then there's the fucking lap dancing ones; don't get me started on those lap dancing photos. If I see that guy who was sitting with a smug smile on his face while Kendal was bent over, I will personally rearrange his face beyond recognition.

When the door opens, my dick goes rock hard at the sight of Kendal. Fucking hell she was beautiful when I last saw her, but now she's absolutely gorgeous and unbelievably sexy. Her red hair that I loved has now gone and replaced by plum, I don't care because she still looks perfect. We just stand there, staring at each other. I let my eyes wander down her body, fucking hell, she looks edible. I want to tear that dress straight off her body.

She clears her throat. "Hi Jax."

She looks nervous. I don't want her to be nervous. "Hey Kendal, you look amazing."

Absolutely fuckable is what my mind is saying. She ducks her head and blushes; wow Kendal blushing! She would have laughed it off four years ago. She closes the door behind her and steps outside. She's close enough now that I can smell her sweet perfume. She walks by my side to the car. A girl this stunning most definitely will be in a relationship; I will have to see to that and put an end to it, because Kendal has always and will always be mine. I open her door and notice a small smile on her lips just as I close the car door behind her. When I get in beside her she's on her phone. I manage to get a little peek and see the words 'Miss you sexy'. Motherfucker, the cheeky son of a bitch has text her while she's out with me.

"Nice car." She looks around at my car nodding her head. I laugh at her; I think she forgets that I know that she knows fuck all about cars.

"It's an Aston Martin DB9 if you want to show off and tell your boyfriend."

Her eyebrows raise, she just looks at me. Shit I've made her angry, but then she smiles. "I don't have a boyfriend."

"Really?"

Her smile widens."Yes, really."

Well, that's made my night. I can't help the fat grin on my face as I drive to the restaurant. I am so thankful that there are no paparazzi hanging about outside. We are immediately shown to our private table. I walk behind Kendal just so I can get a glimpse of that amazing arse. I feel her stiffen as I place my hand on the bottom of her back. I laugh to myself, you better get used to it Kendal, this is the least I want to you do right now. I move my body closer to her, so the men we pass can't admire her as she walks by.

Kendal

Shit! Shit! Shitty shit shit!

Jax looks so much sexier standing in front of me than in his pictures. He's definitely been working out over the past four years. His shoulders look wider and more rounded with muscle. I smile inwardly when I see his hair is in its usual mess. It's also the messy head of hair our son has inherited, which makes my heart melt for this man in front of me. I feel like laughing when I realize that he's not stuck to the dress code for tonight at all. He's wearing tight black skinny jeans. I try and ignore the rush of lust when I notice that his jeans are a little stretched around his crotch area. As my eyes take in the rest of him; my eyes leave his crotch and travel up to his chest, he's wearing a plain white top but it hugs his muscled torso so deliciously. I can see the shape of his pecs and I swallow hard.

He's wearing a black blazer type jacket, but the sleeves, neck collar and lapels are all a black leather material. It hugs his big shoulders and arms. This gorgeous man still affects me so much that I am fighting myself to not just run into his arms right now and have him hold me. My mood is slightly crushed when I got into his ridiculously expensive sports car and read the text I received just as I came out the house. It's from Harley.

HARLEY: *Hi Kendal, I hope we can have that catch up soon because I really do miss U sexy xx*

When Jax got into the car, I quickly put my phone back in my bag and tried to start up a conversation. The only thing I could think of was his car, the truth is, I know fuck all about cars so that was a fail but at least I made Jax laugh.

When we pulled up at Eclipse, I was amazed. I do notice that when we greet the young waitress, while showing us to our table, she's quickly undone the top button of her blouse and adjusts her tits. She turns and flashes her flirtatious smile at Jax, yet she doesn't even acknowledge me. As we follow her, I feel Jax place his hand on the small of my back. My whole body is aware of his hand and his body getting closer to mine. The sparks are still there between us. Four years apart and as soon as we're together again, the pure sexual need returns like we've never been apart.

The young flirtatious waitress, who now keeps looking back to take a peek at Jax, leads us to the far corner of the downstairs seating area to a large elevator. She clicks the button and turns around to face us. Well, I say face us; she only has eyes for Jax. This is another one of the reasons I decided it was time to leave Jax; The females.   Back then, the girls were obvious, but now they're damn well get right in your face. He's standing here, with me and she is still flirting.   She's talking to him whilst fluttering her eyelashes at the same time, and ever so innocently touching his rounded bicep. He still has his hand on my back for crying out loud!

Thankfully the elevator doors open and we both step in leaving the skank outside. She pouts at Jax and then looks back to where she should be standing; obviously torn between doing her job and staying with Jax. "You will be greeted by someone upstairs, or I can come and help you instead?"

I scoff and she gives me an irritated look, then quickly looks back to Jax. Before I can give her a piece of my mind, Jax steps in. "No thanks, I'm here with my very beautiful girl and I don't want to be disturbed."

The elevator doors shut in her face and I burst out laughing. "I'm sorry about that."

I stop laughing and notice that he's frowning down at the floor. I touch his arm and smile at him."Jax, it's fine."

I laugh again, only this time, I'm glad to hear Jax laughing too. That damn sexy deep chuckle of his makes my body shudder. We look at each other and stop laughing. This feels nice. Not awkward at all. I now realize that all of this time while Jax has been out of my life, not only lost my boyfriend but I also lost my best friend.

The doors open to a waiter who is waiting for us. He takes my hand as I step out and gives me a big smile, "Can I show you to your table Miss?"

A hand suddenly touches the lower of my back, I know it's Jax by how my body responds to him. "Yeah, please do."

The man's eyes widen a little and he clears his throat. Jax gently pulls me away from the waiter, we walk side by side. There are about five doors up here and he takes us to the nearest one and opens the door. The room is beautifully decorated in light blue and white, in the middle is a large, white table all set up and ready for us. Jax has hired out a private room for tonight, I look up at him and smile, still not really believing this is happening.

Chapter 18

Jax

Only ten minutes with me and Kendal has already had to deal with that shit. I know they're just fans, but this is one of the reasons Kendal gave me before she ran away from me. I could have killed that jackass who had tried to take her from me when we got out the lift. Kendal is a beautiful woman, so obviously guys will hit on her but not any-more; especially when I'm around.

We have boring chitchat after we order our food, and now Kendal's looking a little awkward sat opposite me. "Thanks for coming with. You didn't have to."

She looks up at me and smiles, but I know it is forced. "That's okay; I came here so it wouldn't be awkward on Saturday."

Well, I was hoping she wanted to see me too. "So, how you been? What have you been doing these past four years?"

She shuffles in her chair a little. "Nothing special, the usual; working and all that. So, tell me about you, I bet your story is more interesting than mine."

"Not really. I just have the guys and Sophie of course. I knew you two would get along."

She nods and puckers her lips, something she does when she is thinking. "I bet you have a lot of girls like her downstairs, all over you."

She's jealous and I know it. Why does she sound angry about it? This is what she wanted."I'm not going to lie about that, but you can't tell me you haven't haven't been with anyone since me."

She blushes and I now feel angry. "Obviously not as many as you."

No, but just the thought of one guy other than me holding her makes me want to kill a bastard. I have no right to, I mean I don't even know the number of women I've slept with. There's been so many.

When the waiter brings our food over it stops me saying anything but I decide to change the subject. We talk about her friends, and she asks me about the guys. I can see by her face she misses them. They miss her too. She looks stunning, I want to hold her like I used to. Naked with no barriers between us. I will have her like that again.

"I can't believe this has all happened."

I nod my head in agreement as I finish my food. "Yeah it's pretty crazy, but it's good to see you Kendal. I always thought about you."

"I thought about you too. I bought all your albums. You really have done great Jax." She blushes and I give her a little wink. When she giggles, the awkwardness lifts. I can't believe after all of this, here she is in front of me. Having dinner looking sexy as sin, all the women I have been with have nothing on this goddess.

The rest of the dinner I shamelessly flirt with her, and when we have dessert I move my chair so that I'm sitting on her side of the table. I place my hand on her knee and I wish I could touch her a lot more, but I need to be on my best behavior.

Kendal

Jax has moved his chair and has his hand is on my knee. My underwear is wet with my arousal with just the feel of his hand on me. All he's done is innocently flirt but I am so horny right now. I finish my dessert and he asks me about my job. "So you're doing what you love?"

"Yes I am finally."

After some innocent flirting I'm aware the atmosphere has changed. He scoots closer and tucks my hair behind my ear. "I'm glad you're doing what you've always wanted to do babe. It makes me happy. We both reached our dreams."

Well, not technically. I wanted to run my own business, but obviously having Finley put a hold on that.

His hand wanders down from my hair and onto my neck. Oh shit. I stare into his beautiful gray eyes. We stare into each other's eyes in silence. I know he can hear my deep lust filled breathing. His eyes go down to my mouth, and I instinctively look at his. Memories of what he's done to me with that mouth are flooding back; I need to stop them. He moves closer and I freeze in place. As much as I want to have his mouth on mine, I can't handle this right now. It's too soon. "Jax."

I whisper and he closes his eyes and then leans his forehead onto mine. "I'm sorry, shall we get you home?"

The drive home is quiet but it's not uncomfortable. It's nice. It's so unreal that I'm here in Jax's car. It's a pity I can't tell him yet, this seems like a good time to tell him but I can't. I'll meet him on Sunday, the sooner the better.

Before I know it, we're outside my house. "Here we are. Thanks for coming."

"I enjoyed it Jax. Thank you."

"Can I ask you a question before you go?"

"Sure, what's up?"

He looks a little shy and then looks right at me with those stunning eyes. "You said that you're not seeing anyone, but who's Finley?"

I gasp. How does he know about Finley? Where did he hear his name?

"Sorry, it's just Sophie said today you were seeing Finley and I was just confused. Forget it, it's not my business."

He sits back in his seat and frowns at his hands on the steering wheel. What can I say?

I suppose I will have to tell him some truth now. It could help towards finally telling him on Sunday. Lessen the blow.

"Finley is my son."

There I said it. Fuck that felt good. I've been scared it was going to slip out all night. Jax doesn't say anything. I look across to him and he looks dazed at his hands that are still on the steering wheel. He looks calm enough but his knuckles are bright white telling me how tight he's gripping it.

"Jax?" Again nothing. "Right well bye."

I get up and fling the car door open in anger. Just before I slam the door shut, I hear him speak. "Does he help you?"

I bend down so I can see him. "Who?"

"The dad."

Fucking hell, think Kendal think! "He doesn't know who his dad is."

He frowns at me. "Do you know?"

I can't believe he just asked me that! What the fuck? "Fuck you Jax. Fuck you!"

I slam the door shut and march up to my garden gate. I can hear

Jax get out of his car and run up to me, but right now, I don't want to look at him.. Fucking cheeky bastard. I feel him lightly grab my elbow. "Kendal, I'm sorry."

I just stand still waiting for him to let me go. "Kenny?"

God, why does he have to use that nickname? I close my eyes and sigh heavily. I open my eyes and catch the blinds moving in my living room window.

"I know who he is but Finley doesn't. He's never met him, and no, he doesn't help, but that's because I chose it to be that way. Happy now?"

"What? No, I'm not happy. How are you coping? Are you okay for money?"

I know he means well but it feels a little insulting. "I'm fine. We're fine. Can I go home now?"

He nods and I can feel his gaze on me as I walk up to my front door and knock. I wait for Jessica to open it but I'm surprised when it's Sam. I feel tears in my eyes and he grabs me in a strong hug and ushers me inside. Jessica takes my hand and leads me into my living room. I'm so upset he would think that of me. We had such a good evening and now this; I only hope it doesn't affect the wedding.

Jax

When I get back home, I go straight to the gym and start punching the punching bag. I am such a fucking idiot! I shout as I punch without the gloves. I don't blame Sam for turning me away from the door. Seeing Kendal crying in his arms made me feel like shit. Why did I ask such a fucked up question?

Of course she would know who her child's father is; I was just being a fuck up as usual. I wanted to follow her into her house and beg for her to forgive me but I was stopped. I could still hear her crying when Sam shut the door in my face. "Didn't go well then?"

I look over my shoulder and see Max standing there leaning against the doorframe.

"No, it was fucking perfect. I just had to fuck it all up right at the end."

"What happened?"

I stop punching and turn to face him. I wipe the sweat out my eyes. "She's got a son, Max." I watch his eyes go wide. "But that's not it."

I tell him everything I had said and I see Max is angry at me for what I said to Kendal. I don't blame him.

"Fucking hell. What are you gonna do?"

"I dunno."

I walk out the gym and know he's following me. "You need to settle it before Saturday."

I get my phone and dial Sophie. She tries to ask questions about how tonight went but I don't say anything. All I want to know is where Kendal works. I have some making up to do.

Chapter 19

Kendal

At work the next day I receive a text from Mark, telling me to look at the paper. On the front page is a picture of Jax and I last night when we were leaving Eclipse. Jax has his arm wrapped around my waist as we walked back to his car. We're both laughing and the picture looks as if we're a happy couple. Jax looks sexy as hell as always but it's the title which grabs my attention.

Jax Spent An Intimate Night With A Local Hottie

A local hottie? I scoff in disbelief and throw it down on the table in the staff room not bothering to read the article.

I've already told Tanya everything from last night. She scowls when I tell her what Jax had to say. To be honest, I was genuinely upset last night but I'm sort of over it now. I'm still trying to get used to the idea Jax, Rhys, Leo and Max are back and that I'm going to see them all tomorrow.

Tanya's more excited than me that my picture is in the paper and I've received texts and missed calls from my parents and friends. I also had a text from Harley too, he thinks I didn't get back to him about his dinner plans with me because I was out with Jax Parker. Yes I was with Jax when I got his text but I didn't reply because he's making me feel weird lately, not because I was with Jax.

Harley thinks I'm disrespectful because we have a history together and I dropped him for someone else, just because they're famous. Obviously he knows nothing about Jax and me because I never told him.

Unlike me, Tanya did read the paper. She lets me know that in the paper they think there is another reason why Jax returned home. They think it's because he's back together with his ex, meaning me.

They say that we're young sweethearts and we have found each other again. They think we are back together and madly in love.

At 11:00 I see a woman walk in with a huge bouquet of flowers, full of red roses and purple tulips. Roses are my favorite flowers but I also know that tulips mean; a declaration of love. Behind her is a younger girl carrying a bag. I'm wondering who the lucky lady is as I watch them both walk to Bianca at the reception area. I'm shocked to see Bianca point at me and then the two women walk towards me. All the women in the salon watch them make their way towards me with huge smiles.

"Kendal Moore?"

"Erm...yes?"

The woman smiles warmly at me. "We have strict orders to make sure you get these before 12:00."

I haven't got a booking for another ten minutes so when I take the flowers and the bag I take them into the staff room. In the bag is an envelope, inside is a hand written letter.

Kendal, I hope you like your gifts. I am so sorry about what I said last night. Please forgive me. I don't know what I'd do if you couldn't. When I saw you in Sam's arms last night I felt like shit, I didn't mean to upset you. I was angry and I took it out on you. I'm not angry that you have a son; to be honest I think that's pretty cool. He's a lucky boy; I just know that you're a great mum. I was angry because the thought of the child's father leaving you to deal with it all on your own pissed me off. I can't believe someone would do that to you. I was jealous, I always thought it would be me and you, a family and all that. I'm glad we had a good time last night; I'm just sorry I spoilt it. Look forward to seeing you again
Love, Your Jax

I read and read it before I even looked in the bag. I put it away safely in my bag. I can understand what happened last night a little better now. I love how he said that I'm a great mum but it also makes me feel sad. He will get to experience being a parent soon enough. I'm looking forward to telling him now, even though I am scared of how he'll take it.

I try not to cry as I take a peek into the bag. There's a big heart shaped box of chocolates, a teddy bear but what makes me tearful is the last item I see. In a silver picture frame is an old photo of us together. Leo's rich step-brother had his own house in Marbella, so one summer I went along with the band. The picture is of Jax and I on the beach, he's standing behind me with arms wrapped around me and his head resting on the side of mine. My bright red hair is blowing in the breeze, and I have a cheesy smile on my face, Jax is grinning too, he looks so happy. I can't believe he still has this photo. I still have it and a lot more but I didn't think Jax would keep them.

It's now 12:00 and I'm in the middle of cutting a girl's hair when I hear Tanya gasp. She's looking towards the door. I quickly turn my head to see what has caused this reaction from her. Standing in the reception area staring at me is Jax. He's wearing gray skinny jeans, black tight t-shirt and fucking hell I can see the shape of his chest and muscles. He's smiling right at me and damn him, that sexy smile of his has does delicious things to my insides. What this man can do to me with just one look. Tanya takes him into the staff room, away from all the girls eyes. When I've finished the customers hair she turns to me with huge wide eyes."Oh my god! You're Jax Parkers girlfriend from the paper. I need a picture with you so I can tell my friends I had my hair cut by Jax Parkers girlfriend!"

I don't bother correcting her, she wasn't joking about the picture. Lucy, a girl I work with, took the photo of us together. When I walk into the staff room, I'm happy to see Tanya guarding Jax.

Bianca has told him I have an hour lunch break today, so Jax wants to take me out for something to eat. He holds my hand as we walk out to his shiny sports car and a few flashes go off across the road but I don't look up. I'm not going to look as pleasant in that snap than the one from last night.

After making a quick stop at a Subway and a short drive Jax pulls up in front of the huge park near my house. It's a massive park, lots of green grass, little lakes darted around the area, trees and bushes separate little private sitting areas and there's a little park where I take Finley. When Jax opens my door, he gives me a shy smile."You don't mind coming here, do you?"

"No I bring Finley here a lot."

"Yeah, I've spent a lot of time here since I've been back. It's nice and quiet."

He holds my hand as he leads me to a secret little bench area surrounded by trees. It's very quiet; I don't think I've been this far into the park before. We dig into our subs and laugh like the good old times. It's nice to see him again and I'm shocked it's so easy to be with him after all this time. I thought it would be awkward, or the fame would have changed him. It's like we're the same old Jax and Kendal.

"I saw your delivery in the staff room."

I grin at him and see he's wearing a cheeky smile. "What can I say? I'm a lucky girl."

"Did you read the letter?"

"Yes, it was lovely Jax. Everything was, you didn't have to do that."

"Yeah I did. I was a dick for what I said to you. I'm sorry Kendal."

"It doesn't matter now, it's all forgotten. OK?"

When we hug, I can't help but breathe him in, he smells so delicious. I don't want to be just friends, I want to be with Jax again like we used to be.. Once I tell him what I have kept from him he will hate me and he won't want anything to do with me.

We slowly walk our way back to his car. It's great that we haven't seen anyone. "Do they follow you everywhere?"

"Yeah, it gets annoying but it comes with the whole package."

He gives me that sexy smile of his and I tell myself over and over 'friends, friends, friends.' We reach his car but he doesn't unlock it straight away; instead he stops walking a few steps away from the door and faces me. Immediately my mantra stops as Jax smiles and softly cups my cheek with his large hand, I can't help but lean into it.

"You're a great girl Kendal, you know that?"

"I'm not that great."

"No, you are. I've missed you so fucking much babe."

He won't be thinking that in a couple of days. He will think I'm a lying bitch. "I've missed you too Jax."

He slowly leans into me and I don't know what to do. Do I? Don't I? We look into each other's eyes and just as his lips are about to touch mine a flash stops us. Jax quickly guides me into his car and slams the door behind me, he's in his seat seconds after I get pushed in and he quickly drives away. "Fuck!"

"Jax it's fine."

"No it is not! You left me because you didn't want all this shit, and it's fucking everywhere."

It was a lie obviously. "It's OK, if they want to get a picture of me while I'm in my work uniform then so be it."

I gesture to my black shorts and purple t-shirt. Jax lifts an eyebrow as he looks over at me when we stop at a traffic light. "I think that uniform is pretty sexy actually."

I laugh, glad that his mood has changed. "Really?"

"Fuck yeah."

Well if that didn't make squirm, I don't know what would. Damn you Jax

Chapter 20

Jax

As soon as I get back from taking Kendal to work I get on the phone to our media manager. Now Kendal has had her photo snapped with me a few times, I need to protect her. I give orders that Kendal is to be known as my ex girlfriend, before we got signed and we've been on and off for years. At least when we get back together we will be safe, because I will get Kendal back.

She looked so happy when I watched her at work. You can tell she loves her job by watching her face. She looked so fucking sexy in her uniform, those black shorts were showing her sexy slim legs, and her purple top clung to her curves and tits. I could see exactly what I've been missing. Kendal sure was shocked to see me, I was just dropping by to see what she thought of the letter and to make sure she forgave me. When her boss sneakily let me know she has an hour lunch break, I had to spend it with her. Nothing fancy, just something like what we used to do. I soon had her laughing and happily chatting away like the good old times. Seeing her face come alive as she spoke about everyone was something I envied. I wish she looked like that when she spoke about me.

As we were about to get into my car I stopped her because I was going to ask if I could meet her son. I'd love to meet him. I don't care if Kendal chose to do this on her own, that's not the thing you do when you get a girl pregnant. You help the mother of your child. I want to help her with Finley, I'd love that. As I spun her around to face me I looked into her eyes and forgot everything I wanted to say. She looked up at me and took me back, she's so fucking beautiful and I wanted to kiss those tempting lips of hers. I would have too if that fucking pap hadn't taken a sneaky picture! I had to get her in the car and out of there fast. Thanks to me, Kendal will probably have to get used to seeing the paparazzi hanging around.

Tomorrow is the wedding, so tonight Rhys is at our house because the girls are over at his place.

"So how did it go this time?" Rhys sits down beside me on the sofa.

"Yeah, amazingly she forgave me. I need her Rhys; I was going to kiss her when a fucking pap started snapping away."

He grimaced, knowing all too well about that. The media are dying to get a better look at Sophie, but Sophie doesn't want them to. She covers herself up and if she was out on her own nobody would know she was Rhys girlfriend. Whereas I've met Kendal twice and we've been caught both times. Max and Leo walk in and thrust a beer in each of our faces.

Kendal

"Are you sure you don't want to come buddy?" I'm tucking Finley into bed at my parents, I feel guilty as hell leaving him again. Sophie understands why it's not a good idea to take Finley to the wedding. He shakes his head dramatically.

"No way mummy. I'm going with Granddad to play with the band. Wedding's are boring."

My dad used to be in a band, nothing big. Just local gigs but they still meet up and play and tomorrow my dad's taking Finley. He loves going and he's taking his little blue guitar I bought him.

When I leave Finley I go straight to Sophie's, it feels weird now coming over when I know it's Rhys' house too. I can't wait to see Max and Leo tomorrow. Jax was my boyfriend; who I was in love with. Rhys was my big older brother and good friend and Leo and Max were like my silly crazy best friends but who also had that protective brotherly side. Most of the time they showed me their love in their own crazy way!   We always had a fun crazy time together.

When I enter the house, Tanya greets me and shoves today's paper in my hand. I take a look and groan. "That's a fucking great picture."

On the front of the paper is the picture that was snapped yesterday, Jax and me at the park. It's a really good picture, I have my head leaning up to his, waiting for Jax to kiss me. Jax has his hands on my body in an intimate way; you can tell that we were having a special moment. "If you think that is bad you should have a look at all the magazines. I had a look on the internet too, you two are the shit on the gossip sites at the minute."

Oh perfect. Tanya just laughs and then leads me through the main entrance and towards the back of the house. I catch my breath when I see the outside. It is truly beautiful, black flooring has been put down to cover the area designed for the wedding. It's a massive area and it still doesn't cover the whole garden. At least women in their heeled shoes won't sink into the grass. Directly in front of where I'm stood, is the walkway Sophie will walk down. On either side are rows of chairs in white fitted covers and a navy sash tied in a big bow at the back. At the end of the walkway is a white archway covered in roses where Sophie and Rhys will be married. It's so classy and cute, so Sophie. On the far left of the garden is a huge marquee and I mean enormous!

"They've done great right? Sophie and Maisy are in there."

We make our way over to the humongous white marquee; no actually it's a tent, a circus tent. When we enter there's a scatter of circular shaped tables with navy table cloth draped over them with chairs the same as the ones outside around them.

Sophie and Maisy are talking near the top table. Sophie runs over and hugs me tight. This is where we will be eating after the ceremony and once the reception starts this is where the DJ will set up and be the main dancing area.

We spend the night very much like when we spent the night

before; full of champagne and giggles. The girls question me over Jax - obviously; Sophie and Maisy are still the romantics and think tomorrow he will make the moves on me. As much as that makes me giddy and hopeful I don't want him to make a move; I just don't think that's a good idea right now.

After a lot of girly chatter, face masks and a huge takeaway meal, Sophie shows us to where we will be sleeping. She opens a door and it's all white apart from the pink sheets on the two double beds, I'm so happy to see we're staying in the same room. On one side of the girly sleepover room are the four black dress bags with our names in italic pink writing. While the girls get ready for bed and unpack, I go and call my dad to check up on Finley.

"Hey kiddo." I love hearing my dad's deep voice; it makes me feel like I'm home.

"Hey dad, how is Fin?"

"Still asleep. How is it going over there?"

"A lot of fun."

There's a silence and for some unknown reason I'm scared. *"Listen, we know that your friend is getting married to Rhys. Your mum and I have seen the papers. Just tell me the truth; is Jax Parker Finley's dad?"*

Fucking hell, I knew I should have told them first. We shouldn't be doing this over the phone, but he's asked me for the truth. "Yeah its true dad, we met when I was in college. I found out I was pregnant and decided not to tell him and leave him. I know it was a shit thing to do dad but I couldn't end his dream before it began. I rea-"

"Kendal, stop." I stop and wait for it. *"I can understand what you did but it doesn't mean it was a good idea. You're going to have to tell him Kendal, we will talk more when I see you OK?"*

"Okay dad."

"Alright, I'll see you in the morning."

I stare at my phone after I hang up and get a hold of myself.

Chapter 21

"Remember my cake mummy." I smile at my gorgeous son. I've just spent three hours at my parent's house with Finley before I start getting ready for the wedding. I think he's mentioned wedding cake about ten times since I've been here. "I won't forget the cake Fin."

"That's good because I like cake." I give Finley about a thousand kisses, when I get into my car I see I have a text from Jessica.

JESSICA: Remember 2 get the pics from mine

The woman hasn't even given me the chance to forget the pictures for Sophie. When I return to Sophie's, Tanya grabs me by the arm and leads me upstairs. "Thank god you're here. Sophie's a nervous wreck."

She takes me to a big room, music is quietly playing in the background. Sophie walks in with her huge white dress bag and orders us to go and shower before we have breakfast. After a very quick shower, I wrap myself in the white dressing gown and dry my hair upside down. I grab my dress bag and gather my makeup and everything I need for my hair. Once I return to the bridal room I'm hounded into drying Jessica's hair."You know you could do this yourself."

She making a snorting sound."When I have a friend who is a hairdresser?"

When Sophie walks in a kindly offer to dry her hair, sticking my tongue out at Jessica. When we all have dried hair we make our way to the dining room and eagerly eat our late breakfast. I hear a low snuffle and look to my left, Sophie is wiping away a few tears."Ohhh Soph."

I wrap my arms around her and she laughs a little. "Oh don't mind me. I'm just all emotional today."

Jessica grips her shoulder on her other side. "It's your wedding day. It is against the law not to cry on your wedding day."

Jessica and Maisy disappear as Tanya and I talk excitedly about today to keep her distracted from asking where they have gone. When they return they're holding three large red bags and a long box. The bags are huge, Tanya and I get up and take a gift each.

"I didn't expect you to get me anything."

Jessica and Maisy lay their big bags on the table in front of Sophie. She reaches for one and pulls out four A4 sized gift wrapped boxes. She rips the first one along the top and gasps, placing her hand over her mouth. We all see her teary eyes and stand closer so we can see which one she has opened. The one she has opened is a beautiful picture of us standing with our backs to the camera looking out at the sea in Barcelona. Sophie's in the middle with the sun shining above. Sophie looks up to us all with awe. "Oh my god guys, I love it." Her voice breaks a little as she speaks.

"Well, you still have more to open."

Tanya laughs and Sophie grabs another gift eagerly. This one if from my camera. We're all on the yacht and lying on our stomachs in our bikinis, hand on our chins and legs crisscrossed behind us with our feet in the air. We're all smiling big cheesy grins with the view of the ocean behind us. The third is the picture we asked the waiter in the hotel to take of us before we all went out clubbing on the last night, the fourth is a picture of us in the sea splashing and laughing. She sets them down in a large square. "I love these girls, they're beautiful."

"Don't thank us yet, you have more."

Jessica gives her the other red bag on the table. These last two pictures are not wrapped. She slides the first one out of the bag and smiles. "Oh my god! I can remember us all laughing at Sophia making us do this one."

Sophia had lain down on the sand with her camera pointed up to the sky. She told us all to stand around her and lean over the camera. It felt really silly and we were all laughing. It made a fabulous picture with our heads huddled in a circle, hair falling down our happy faces with the sun and bright blue sky peeking out behind our heads.

I hand her the last canvas print. We all wanted her to have this one last as it is our favorite picture and by the look on her face she loves it too. "Wow."

It's like the other picture of us where we have our backs to the camera on the beach but on this one we're facing the camera. We're all laughing towards the camera, barefoot and in our beach wear. "Girls I love them."

Tanya reminds us that we're not done. "There's one big present left that I'm sure Rhys will love."

We move away so Tanya can pass her the long present. When she realizes what it is, she bursts out laughing. "Let me guess, this was Tanya's idea."

"Obviously."

"Yeah, he will definitely love this present."

Inside the box is a dancing pole, a great gift if you ask me. When it is 11:00am we go on back to the bridal room to get ready.

Chapter 22

While Tanya and I were busy styling Jessica and Maisy's hair, Sophie had turned the music louder and started on her own make-up. Jessica and Maisy are sitting down at two of the dressing tables busy doing their make-up while I'm doing Sophie's hair. I give her soft curls and add a little poof at the top with a little sparkly clip to secure it.

I'm getting the bride ready, which is one of my best friends and I'm spending the whole day with my ex who I still love and is the father of my son. Weddings just make me emotional anyway, never mind the added turmoil and I start to feel a little emotional.

"Oh Soph, you look so beautiful." I feel the tears coming and I try my best to hide them.

"Don't you dare Kendal, don't you start crying, not yet."

I fan my tears away that are dangerously close to falling and turn away from her. Tanya and I do each other's hair and then make a start on our make-up.

I've just finished my make-up when there's a loud knock on the door. Jessica goes to answer it and in walks a pretty woman who looks like she's in her mid-twenties, tall and skinny with long blonde hair. She's really pretty and standing beside her is a cute mini version, obviously mother and daughter. I think of my little boy back at my parents' house.

"Steph!" Sophie quickly walks over to the woman and young girl to give them a hug. "Girls, this is my sister-in-law Steph, Rex's wife and their daughter Milly, who is the flower girl." Milly is very quiet, but she's excited when she spots her small white dress hanging up beside ours. "These are my four best friends and bridesmaids; Kendal, Tanya, Maisy and Jessica."

When Milly has spent ten minutes with us, she comes out of her shy little shell. Tanya curls her golden hair into adorable loose curls. Her mum sits her down on a chair to play on her Nintendo DS while she gets herself ready. I look at Milly happily quiet and playing and Steph gives me a knowing look and laughs. "I know that look, do you have a child?"

"Yes, his name is Finley."

" That DS has saved me a lot of headaches."

I look back to Milly smiling at her game. "I bet it has."

She laughs and sits down at the empty dressing table beside me. I think I just found Finley's birthday present.

Sophie holds out a glass of champagne for me and I happily take it. I need some courage to help me face Jax."Okay girls, let's get you into your dresses."

Jessica wiggles her finger in Sophie's face, making Milly laugh. "The bride goes first and then the bridesmaids."

Tanya and Maisy run to where the huge white dress bag is hanging. They slowly unzip the bag and we all watch as they carefully take the dress out. They hang it next to the floor length mirrors and we all drift closer to the beautiful dress. Sophie lightly touches her dress and then turns to face us with shiny eyes.

Maisy places her hands on her shoulders. "Come on. Let's get you into your dress before we all start to cry."

She takes her dressing gown off and while we wolf whistle at the sight of Sophie in her sexy white lace bridal underwear. She slips into her sparkly heels first, I hold the dress open for her near the floor so she can step in while Jessica holds her hand to steady her. I slowly pull it over her body, careful not to snag anything. Jessica zips the back and I fluff out the bottom of the dress. We all step back and admire her.

"How do I look?"

We all speak at once.

"Beautiful"

"Gorgeous"

"Stunning"

"Sexy."

Sophie grins at her reflection in the mirrors and twirls like a five year old would do in a princess dress. Milly takes her eyes away from her DS and stares with wide eyes at Sophie. "Wow auntie Sophie! You're a princess!"

We're all smiling like idiots and cooing over Milly admiring Sophie. To Milly she's a real life Disney princess come to life.

When Sophie orders us all to get in our own dresses we all eagerly rush to get into our beautiful dresses. I don't know about the girls but I'm so excited to finally get into my dress. All ready, we stand in front of Sophie waiting for her to speak but she just stands there silent."Oh girls, you're going to make me cry."

We all laugh and fight our tears away.

There's a knock on the door, nobody seems to move so I decide to answer it. When I open the door and see who it is, I freeze on the spot. My two long lost crazy best friends. I knew I would see them today but knowing and seeing them is totally different.

Max and Leo look as handsome as ever, looking adorable in their suits, even if they do look slightly uncomfortable. They look exactly as they always have done but with a few added muscles, tattoos and piercings

Leo has his signature blonde hair that always looks like he ran his hand through it and his bright blue eyes. Max has dark brown hair that is short but if you ran your hand through it you could still grab some hair, his hazel eyes have always been my favorite part of him because they stand out.They're both standing side by side and are looking at me with huge smiles. God, I've missed seeing these guys! Leo holds out his arms to me.

"Are you gonna stand there grinning at me all day or are you gonna give me a hug Kenny?" I don't even think twice about it, the door slams behind me as I run into his arms. I bury my face in his neck. "It's good to see you baby girl."

I look up to see his face and I'm sure I can see a trace of water in his eyes."I've missed you Leo."

He kisses my forehead and I feel someone grip my arm. "Stop keeping her to yourself."
I giggle as Max snatches me away from Leo. He grabs me tightly in his arms and I think I can feel him sniffing my hair. "You don't know how much I've missed you."

I love both Leo and Max, I was so close to both of them. I love James, Sam, and Mark but Max and Leo are something else. They know how to show me a good time. They're my brothers who were more like my best friends. I can't put it into words but I do know I love these guys and I'm so happy to see them. Max sets me back at arm's length but his hands still have a hold on my shoulders. "Let me look at you."

I feel a little nervous as they're both stare at me. "What?"

They both lower their heads and chuckle. "Fucking hell Kendal, why did you have to go fall in love with Jax?"

I giggle and shove Max's hands off me and step back. "Shut up Max."

Leo rubs his face with his palms. "I can't believe you're here."

He grabs me in a tight hug again. I laugh against his chest, and he kisses my hair. "I love the new hair too."

I stand back again and cross my arms over my chest. The subject of my hair is a little tender, seeing as the reason I originally dyed it purple was because I wanted a change from Jax. He always told me he loved my red hair.

"Erm, thanks."
,
Max, ever so protective, steps closer and lifts my chin with his finger. When my eyes meet his, I see he doesn't look happy and he's frowning down at me. "What's the matter?"

Before I can answer, I hear the thumping of fast feet coming up the stairs and stop next to us. Max drops the grip he has on my chin. I turn and see Rhys and a very unhappy looking Jax. What's up with him?

Rhys is smiling at me, last time I saw him I freaked out a little. Well a lot, so I think I make up for it when he takes a step towards me but I run towards him. He laughs and wraps his arms around me. "You look good Kendal."

"Thank you."

"I don't mean the dress, I mean you."

What do I say to that? I break away and see Jax looking at me, thankfully looking happier. Can I hug Jax? I feel like shit if I don't because I just hugged his three best friends. I slowly step towards him but he stalks over to me and wraps me in his big strong arms. I sigh from feeling a little relieved, finally in his arms. I can't count the amount of times I've thought about being in this man's arms again. I feel him groan against me and it snaps me out of it. I quickly pull away from his arms feeling a little dazed. I clear my throat "Hi Jax."

He smiles sweetly at me. "You look beautiful."

"Thank you."

I feel the guys come closer and Max clears his throat. "Erm I'll speak to ya later."

I nod and they all salute their goodbyes to me. They obviously want to give us some alone time.

Jax looks sexy as sin in his suit. I look down at his feet and laugh at his Converse. "Did none of you guys want to wear shoes?"

He scrunches up his face looking a little disgusted. "Can you really see us in shoes?"

"Probably not. You look good in a suit." Too good actually, I just want to rip it off his body.

"Not as good as you in that dress. You look amazing babe."

He steps closer and strokes my arm that is now covered in goose bumps. His hand travels up my arms and onto my neck. I look into his beautiful gray eyes. As he leans forward I hear the bridal room door open and I step away from Jax, the spell now broken. I look and see Tanya standing there with her eyebrows raised."Hi Jax."

Jax turns and goes to give Tanya a friendly hug. "Tanya, it's good to see you."

"Good to see you too, Kendal. We need to finish up."

That's me being summoned back into the safety zone.

Chapter 23

Jax

As soon as Rhys told me that Leo and Max had gone to see Kendal, I ran straight up there too. I hated the thought of them seeing Kendal without me, childish but I don't fucking care.

When I saw Max holding onto her, talking to her quietly, I wanted to kill him. I know they're just friends and Max would never betray me like that. It still hurt seeing Kendal so close to Max when she hasn't even hugged me since seeing her. They break apart and I'm taken back by how gorgeous she looks. As soon as she took that one step towards me, I knew what she wanted and I closed the distance and held her in my arms. I couldn't help the groan that escaped me when I felt her sexy little body against mine. It's been too long.

I like that she seemed to take in my appearance, I can't help but pull her towards me just to be closer. Those lips of hers tempt me but as soon as the door behind me opens, she breaks away. For fuck sake, I can't catch a break! Every time I come close, something happens.

I turn to see it's the feisty little Tanya. When Kendal walks into the room I look at her magnificent legs! If those are not fuck me shoes, I don't know what they are. Tanya give me a knowing look and she shakes her head before closing the door.

When I go back downstairs Rhys waves me over. It's time to stand in our places. I can't stop thinking about Kendal. She's even more beautiful than I remembered. She seems different too. My feelings for her came running back to me as soon as I saw her and it shocked me a bit how strong they were so quick.

When we're stood by Rhys at the front, Leo leans into me. "Is

Tanya here?"

"All of them are here."

Rhys turns around to look at me."Are you gonna be alright today?"

"Yeah sure."

Kendal

Sophie is holding onto her dad tightly, I'm directly behind Sophie alongside Jessica. She grabs onto my hand and gives it a reassuring squeeze. The music starts and the voices outside all stop, waiting for the bride. Sophie gives Milly a kiss before she slowly makes her way down the aisle, sprinkling rose petals as she walks. Sophie turns to face us all, still gripping onto her dads arm. "Right girls, this is it."

She beams a big smile but her bottom lip is quivering. Sophie's dad wipes at his face and clears his throat. "Come on girls; let's not mess those pretty faces."

We laugh at him and collect ourselves, it's time to walk down the aisle. I hold my flowers in one hand, still holding onto Jessica's hand with the other. We both look to each other and smile. As long as I have my girls I'll be fine. I relax a little and look up. I look right into the eyes of Jax but I can't look at him for too long right now. I look to Rhys and I feel so happy for him. His eyes are filled with so much love as he watches Sophie make her way down to him.

Before I cry I look at Leo, who gives me a wink. He then looks directly behind me at Tanya with a strange look. I look back to Jax, I look into his eyes and my heart pounds so hard. His eyes tear at my heartstrings, he's looking at me the same way Rhys is at Sophie.

I shake as I keep eye contact with him until I can't look at him anymore. I stand behind Sophie as her dad places her hand in Rhys'. When I hear Sophie crying my tears start to fall too. I'm so happy for them, I hear Rhys' voice break as he repeats his vows to Sophie. I can't fight the emotion anymore. I look behind me and see Maisy, Tanya and Jessica are crying just like me.

Chapter 24

Jax

I see Sophie walking down the aisle looking so beautiful. I'm so happy for these two, happy that my best friend found the love I had found in Kendal but lucky for him that he didn't lose Sophie. Rhys used to be just like Leo and Max until he set his eyes on Sophie. Hell, I used to be like Leo and Max until I met Kendal. We met at a mutual friend's house party where Decoy was playing. I spotted her bright red hair first and then I watched her for the rest of the night. She was eighteen and I was twenty. As soon as I spoke to her that was it. She had me and I had to have her. Kendal was by far the sexiest girl I had ever seen and I couldn't see any other girl ever comparing to her ever again. It's still like that now, I've not met another girl as beautiful as she is and as I watch Kendal walk behind Sophie it's like I'm back at that party. I see nobody else, only Kendal. I can't take my eyes off her, she looks amazing.

Her eyes lock straight onto mine, I keep my hold on her as she walks closer, watching her as she struggles to hold onto me.

I can see her as she watches Sophie and Rhys. Her eyes are wide and wet. She's biting on her lip which is what she does when she fights her emotions. I see her wipe a tear away but when Sophie starts to cry Kendal's tears fall. When they lean in to kiss, I wink at Kendal who's looking at me now and she laughs. I see the ice break around her and I grin back. I get to spend the whole day with Kendal today. Maybe not with her by her side but I can see her, creepy as that sounds.

Sophie and Rhys start to walk back up the aisle and I realize that all the best men and bridesmaids all walk out side by side and it's just my luck I'm walking down with Kendal. She gives me a happy smile. The meal is next, I can't go through it and the speech without talking to her again. As soon as we walk back through the doors I take hold of her hand and lead her into a private room. I want Kendal back, I don't want what Leo and Max have. I want what Rhys has.

"Jax, what are you doing?" She looks a little alarmed when I shut the door behind me. She's biting hard on that gorgeous mouth of hers.

"I just need to talk to you before we eat."

She licks her lips and I hold in a groan. No sex plus seeing Kendal equals horny Jax.

"Okay, what do you need to talk about?"

I swallow hard trying to wet my suddenly dry throat. "Why did you leave me Kendal?"

She looks down to her feet and I feel like shit. I shouldn't have just thrown it out there like that. I take a couple of steps toward her and I'm about to tell her don't answer but she interrupts me. "Look, I can't tell you now, but I will."

I take some more steps closer, so I'm standing right in front of her. "You can tell me now."

She shakes her head fast, still looking towards the floor. What's the matter with her? I hold onto her face with a hand on each side of her head. She looks like she's going to cry. "I can't Jax. Not here, not today."

"Kendal you can tell me anything."

"I will, tomorrow. Come to my house tomorrow." She straightens up and holds her head high. She wants to go but I want some more alone time with her. I bring my face closer to hers and she whispers softly. "Jax."

I need to kiss her. I want her so bad. I brush my lips against hers then I feel her hands on my chest and see her close her eyes. I don't even hear the door open. "Jax!"

Standing in the doorway are Max and Jessica. I let go of Kendal and whisper to her. "I need you back Kendal."

And then I walk out the door.

Kendal

God I wished I had grabbed his face and kissed him, but I didn't. When Max and Jessica came bursting into the room I don't know if I'm angry with them or relieved. Nothing could have prepared me for what he said to me. He wants me back? When he hears what I have to say tomorrow he won't want me anymore.

Max follows after Jax, but Jessica comes straight to me and gives a much-needed hug. I was so scared that he would push too hard and I would come out with it. Today is an emotional day and I do really want to tell him. I can't let a bomb drop like that here, not on Rhys and Sophie's day.

"I saw him take you away, I tried to come in sooner but Max said to give you a few. You okay?"

"Yeah I'm fine. I was just scared I was going to say too much."

"Not long now honey."

We walk out the room Jax took me to and into the room we were in before the ceremony began. All the wedding party is in here while the guests walk over to the marquee.

"I still love him Jess." I whisper and hang my head low.

"Of course you still love him, you didn't stop."

This is so bloody hard! Sophie is approaching us so I try and calm down. "Hey, you okay?"

I smile and nod my head. Rhys stands by Sophie and kisses her on her cheek. "Kendal, can we talk?"

Sophie and Jessica silently walk away together.

"You okay?"

"Yeah."

"Are you staying?"

"Of course, I'm not going anywhere."

He grabs me into a big comforting hug. I've really missed Rhys. I didn't realize how much until now, all I always thought about was Jax and Finley. It wasn't until now, in his arms, that I feel like I have my big brother Rhys back. If you ever had to design the big brother you wanted, I'm pretty sure everyone would have a Rhys. "Why did you leave Kendal?"

He holds me back by the shoulders to look at me when I don't answer. "He said you couldn't take the girls and all the attention. I know that's not true."

He gives me that disapproving look. "What's the real reason Kendal? I tried calling but I couldn't get through and you wasn't at home."

That's because I chucked my phone away. They didn't know where Maisy lived so I stayed with her for a while until I knew they were out of town. "He didn't need me keeping him back Rhys."

He cocks his head to the side and frowns at me again. "I don't believe a word of that. He still loves you."

"She still loves him too."

I gasp when I hear Jessica behind me. I turn to give her my traitor glare. "Jess, shut up!"

I do the whisper shout at her. She shakes her head and Sophie's standing beside her not knowing what to do. Why can't everyone just stop and enjoy their wedding day?

"Kendal it's true, so stop trying to hide it." She walks right up to me. Obviously my glare has not put her off from coming near me. She looks up to Rhys and I know she has now moved onto Sophie and Maisy's side. "Since the day she left him she's been miserable. She tried to move on but it didn't work out. Last year her ex asked her to move in with him and she couldn't because she can't commit to anyone else."

Maisy stands by Jessica, not looking at me at all. I might as well not be here. "And seriously, Harley was hot. If she could have moved on, it should have been Harley. But she couldn't."

I look down to my shoes. Wishing and praying to be somewhere else, anywhere but this awkward conversation. Everything that is being said is true. Jessica the traitor looks to me. "Just tell Jax you still love him."

"You do?"I freeze. Jax heard that? I wish the floor would swallow me up now.

Rhys is shaking his head but he's smiling, totally ignoring that Jax just interrupted us. "Sounds just like Jax. He tried and failed because of Kendal."

Why is everyone talking about my love life like I'm not even standing here? I feel someone grab my hands and I look up to see Jax. He looks straight into my eyes."It's true. I still love you, I need you back."

"I-I can't do this right now." I'm shaking like crazy, I leave them standing there. They can carry on talking about me. I'll deal with

Jess later. I hear Rhys say 'let her go', probably to Jax. I can't believe he still loves me. After four years and now his fame he still loves me. I can't ignore the stab in my heart thinking of him with other girls, but I tried to move on too. I failed, but I can't be mad at him for trying too.

I can't believe Jax heard what Jessica said either. Maybe she said it because she knew Jax was there?

I need some fresh air so I walk back through the double doors. Everyone's happily talking and making their way into the marquee that should really be called a circus tent it's that big. I just need five minutes to clear my head. I'll be in that circus tent soon and so will Jax. I come outside and see Max and Leo leaning against the house. Maybe I can sneak off in the other direction but Leo notices me and he starts to smile at me but then it falls into a frown."What's up Kendal?"

He pushes off the wall and walks up to me. Max joins him looking just as concerned.

"Just need a breather."They both raise an eyebrow."Everyone is talking about me like I'm not even here!"

Max places a hand on my shoulder."Yeah well, this is a fucked up situation."

"So what have you been up to?"

I shrug my shoulders but I'm thankful Leo hasn't asked me about Jax."The usual."

Again Leo raises his pierced eyebrow."Well, I don't know what the usual is anymore."

"I'm sorry, I wanted him to have what you guys have; music and girls."

They both scrunch their faces up. "Wow Kendal that is crazy talk.

You think he wants cheap and easy pussy when he had you? They have nothing on you. Surely you saw that or are you blind?"

I hang my head in shame. I hear a smack and look up see to Leo holding the back of his head. "Back off Leo, she's just had all these same questions in there." Max takes me into a hug and then releases me. "Do I see new piercings?"

I laugh and it feels good."Yeah, I've had my tragus, tongue and erm, my nipple done since I last saw you."

I can feel my face heating. I shouldn't have told them that."That's very sexy Kendal. Any tats yet?"

"I might have Finley's name sometime soon."They both nod."Did Jax tell you?"

"Yeah, and he also told us that you're alone."

Leo looks to Max and frowns and then looks back to me."I didn't know that you were alone Kendal. Why isn't Finley's dad around?"

"Who is it? I'll knock the fucker out."

"Look, it's fine OK?"

I see Tanya and Maisy walking out to me. Tanya places her hand on my arm and I know it's a silent question to ask if I'm okay, so I give her a nod back. "Everyone's sitting down for the meal, you coming?"

I turn and see Jax, Rhys, Sophie and Jessica walking towards us. As soon as I see Sophie and Rhys I feel like shit. This is spoiling their day. I give Sophie a tight hug when she's close enough.

"I'm sorry about this Soph." I whisper in her ear and she squeezes me and whispers back.

"Don't be silly, let's get drunk later and forget it all."

Rhys pats my head and I see Jessica getting closer to me but give her a glare that stops her in her tracks."Kendal"

I shake my head ignoring her sad tone. "I want a strong drink before I talk to you Jess."

I walk away and leave her standing with everyone else. I see on the board at the entrance that shows the seating plan that the bridesmaids and Leo and Max are on the table right near the top table. Thankfully, Jax is on the top table but he's still right in my view. I sit at our table and Tanya and Maisy go to the bar that's set up at the far end. This is turning out to be a very stressful and confusing day. The girls return with drinks at the same time as Jess walks in with Leo and Max. She sits right next to me and I take big gulps of the drink Tanya sets in front of me. I don't want to be mad, but I can't believe she outed me and my feelings like that. Jax walks by and takes his seat at the top table.

Jessica puts her hand on my leg and I look at her sad face. "I'm sorry Kendal. I can see by how Jax looks at you that he loves you. I just want you happy. Hug?" I fall into her open arms. "Let's just have fun today and worry tomorrow."

I can't argue with that.

Chapter 25

Jax

I've been watching Kendal as she talks with Rhys. When I see Jessica approach I gravitate towards them. When I get close enough, I hear everything Jessica says. I don't care that Rhys tells her my feelings because I've already told Kendal I want her back. If she loved me, then why did Kendal leave me? I don't buy all the crap she fed me four years ago anymore.

When I speak up I see Kendal stiffen. I walk right up to her and tell her it's all true. She's biting that lip of hers again, trying to fight her emotions. "I-I can't do this right now."

She quickly walks away from me, so I start to go after her but Rhys catches my arm "Let her go man."

"I need to talk to her."

"She needs space."

I stand there as she walks away. Rhys and Sophie leave me and Jessica standing side by side. "It's good to see you Jax."

"You too Jess." I look from where Kendal has gone outside and to Jessica. "How has Kendal really been, Jess?"

She frowns at my question. "She's been okay. Finley keeps her happy. He's the only good part that's happened out of all this."

"What do you mean?"

Her cheeks blush a little."Erm, it's just that he keeps Kendal happy."

Okaayy, that was a little awkward and I don't know why. "Is it true Jess?"

Jessica smiles at me sadly."Everything I said is true Jax and by looking at you, I'd say you look as miserable as Kendal."

"You can tell huh?"

"I'm not blind Jax! I've seen how you look at her. You haven't stopped looking at her since she walked down that aisle. She still loves you and she's going to kill me for telling you for all of this but it's all true. I'm sick of seeing her unhappy. The thing is she left you because she loves you, as stupid as that sounds."

"That doesn't make any sense." If you love someone you stay with them, you do not leave them. I never wanted to leave her. She obviously didn't feel the same as me.

"You don't understand. She stood on the sidelines, watching you four get more popular by the day. That meant more groupies. She knew this was your dream before you met her. The band, the fame, and the girls that come along with rock stars. She thought she was keeping you from living the dream you always dreamt of, keeping you back. So she left you to live that dream."

I'm stunned. She left me because she thought my dream included the girls? When we first started, the girls were a bonus but as soon as I met Kendal that all changed. I wanted nothing to do with other girls because I had my gorgeous Kendal. She added to my dream. Did Kendal really see herself like that?

"Jess, I didn't want the girls. I had **the** girl. **My** girl. I never fucking forgot her. I think about her every day. I can't let her go again. If she loves me, I'm fighting for her. She can't get rid of me again."

Jessica starts to cry but she is smiling at me."Please don't give up on her Jax. I want her to be happy. I didn't realize how much she loved you but seeing her without you these four years it's obvious. She loves you, please don't let her go. No matter what

Jax, fight for her please."

I feel like there's more she wants to say to me, but Sophie and Rhys come back. It's time to eat and when we walk outside I see Kendal. She's talking to Tanya and Maisy. Jessica tries to approach Kendal but by the look she just threw at her I wouldn't go near Kendal either. She looks pissed and I can't help but feel sorry for Jessica. Kendal's too hurt to see that Jess is just trying to help her. When Kendal storms off with Tanya and Maisy behind her, I say sorry to Jessica. "Don't worry, she will forgive me. She loves me too much."

She smiles but I can see she's hurting. Max and Leo walk up to me, Leo has a fat smirk on her face."So, I had a chat with Kendal."

I cringe. "What did you say to her?"

"Well we talked and she told us where she lived. Unlike you did. Max told her that she was blind to not see you only wanted her pussy and no-"

I cut him off and glared at Max. "You fucking said that?"

Someone fucking give me a break here. Max shrugs. Oh just great. Sophie and Jessica are laughing.

"Kendal has had some new piercings since she left."Max wiggles his eyebrows at me.

"Yeah, I think you will especially enjoy two of them."What are they talking about? I frown at them, I'm angry they talked about me and pussy with Kendal. Leo huffs out loud and comes closer so he can whisper in my ear."She's gotten her tongue and nipple done."

I feel my eyes widen. Fuck. I used to love her little belly button bar but now these! I'd love to see her sexy little nipple and I'm dying to feel what that tongue now feels on my cock. It's growing just thinking about it. Sophie's still laughing when she tells us it is time to go and sit down.

Kendal

During the delicious meal, Leo and Max have been making us all laugh and I'm beginning to relax. As the dessert dishes are taken away, Max taps me on the shoulder."Can you remember our song Kenny?"

I laugh in embarrassment, I do remember. If Max and I were out together and we heard Nickelback's song *Rock star*, we would dance and sing every word. It quickly became our song. "How could I forget?"

"Yeah well if it comes on later I'm coming to find you. You can't sing our song without me."

"Deal."

Max wraps his arm around my back and leans in close. "Kendal, since you left he hasn't moved on. I'm not gonna lie, he did try. I know he still loves you."

The thought of Jax being with someone hurts, but that's my fault. "Max, I just wanna have fun today okay? All this serious shit can wait until after the wedding."

I have a quick peek at Jax who is looking right back at me so I quickly look away.Sophie's dad makes his father of the bride speech, which makes most of the women here cry. It was so emotional, I'm so glad I have waterproof mascara on. Sophie stands next and I can tell she's a little nervous.

"I know the bride doesn't usually make a speech but I just wanted to thank you for all coming. I want to separately thank Rex, Jax, Leo, and Max for for returning Rhys to me safe and in one piece." There's a chorus of laughter and Max and Leo raise their drinks to

Sophie. "Next, I want to say thank you to our beautiful little niece Milly, our flower girl. Milly, we have a little present or you."

Milly bounces up to the top table and Rhys gives her a kiss and hands her a big Disney Princess bag that's full of goodies. She struggles a little so Rex gets up to help her. By the looks of her huge smile, she's a very happy girl.

"Thank you to my four amazing bridesmaids. They're not just my best friends, they're my sisters, I really love you girls. Maisy helped me transform our house. Jessica helped with all the treats and the wedding cakes. Trust me, they're delicious! Tanya and Kendal, who I kept very busy this morning. The bonus to having hairdressers and beauticians as your best friends gave them the job of making us all look beautiful for today. You all look gorgeous, don't they guys?"

Wolf whistles fill the room. Tanya, Maisy, Jessica, and I all look at each other and giggle. Max shouts,"Damn right"

Leo follows looking straight at Tanya when he shouts, "Sexy."

That statement makes her duck her head and blush even more which is very unlike Tanya. Maisy and Jessica think so too as we all share a knowing look.

"My girls gave me an amazing hen trip too. Two nights in sunny Barcelona! We got drunk in the sun and had a party on a yacht. We had some very useful lessons that I can show Rhys tonight thanks to one of their wedding presents for Rhys and I."

Rhys looks confused and we're all giggling. "Thank you to my amazing husband Rhys who has made my life perfect. When you asked me to marry you, I didn't think I could be happier but today has topped that."She wipes tears from her eyes and I do too, her voice cracks when she looks down at Rhys."I love you so much."

Rhys stands to hold her and through the microphone that's been placed on the top table we all hear Rhys."You make me so happy baby."

Jessica shoves a handful of tissues in my face, I'm so grateful because I'm a blubbering mess. As Rex walks up to the top table to give his embarrassing big brother speech, Max leans forward into the table and whispers to me and the girls. "Girl's, what's the lesson Sophie was talking about?"

We all laugh but I want to see his reaction. "We all had lap dancing and pole dancing lessons in Barcelona."

Oh wow, the look on his face is priceless. "So what is the present you guys got them?"

I turn to Leo with a mischievous smile on my face. "It was Tanya's idea to get them a dancing pole for their bedroom."

His eyes go wide and his eyebrows shoot up. I look at Max and he looks the same, they look so funny. Leo looks at Tanya with a very intense look and his eyes look heavy with lust and even I blush. What is with these two? I thought they hated each other.

I hear clapping and I see Rex sitting down from his speech. Jax stands up, I forgot he was making a speech! How can a man be that sexy? His thick black hair looks tidier today and I can see the shine from the gold hoop in his ear. He also has his right eyebrow and his bottom lip pierced too adding to his sexy rocker look. His deep voice comes through the speakers as he speaks into the microphone and it sends chills all over my body.

"Hey guys, I'm Jax, one of the best men. I met Rhys when we were fourteen, I'm so happy to see he's found Sophie. I can see that you're made for each other. Everyone in this room can see that. Ever since we had our first guitar lesson we shared a dream of starting our own band and playing in front of our fans. What we both didn't realize is that the dream is not worth living if you're not surrounded by the people you love and who know the real you. Our crazy life can be hard and Rhys has Sophie to welcome him home after a day of people just looking at the band side of you. It's good to have a good woman who knows the real you. I'm very jealous Rhys."

He glances my way and I swear my heart stopped beating. He looks back to the happy couple, everyone at my table is quiet. "Rhys, do everything you can to make your girl happy, because to be honest, we can't figure out how the hell you managed to get such a beautiful woman to fall in love with you."

People laugh but I'm not one of them and I feel Jessica grip my hand. Tears are lingering in my eyes. "Seriously I love you guys, I'm so happy for you both."

He sits down and he smiles around at everyone but when he looks at me he gives me the sweetest smile, almost as if it's a shy smile. I cannot help but smile back. It really is scary how much father and son look like each other.

Chapter 26

Jax

It's time for Rhys' speech, so I take my eyes from Kendal and look at my best friend.

"Thank you to everyone who came today. Thank you Milly for being our little princess today and to our incredibly gorgeous bridesmaids, we love you all. My wife, Jax is right you're way too good for me Soph. I'm so lucky you walked into my life, the fact you put up with my crazy lifestyle and messy habits is amazing. Every day I wake up and see you next me, I realize I'm not in a dream. You're mine, and it blows my mind. I can't wait to start a family, you're going to be the best mother a child could ask for and I will be right by your side. When you agreed to travel around with the band and then move in with me, I couldn't be happier. It wasn't until I saw you looking walking towards me, down that aisle that it actually sunk in. You are going to be my wife. You've taken my breath away today and I'm sure you will do for the rest of our lives."

Rhys pulls a sobbing Sophie up into his arms. The soppy bastard, I thought I acted bad when it came to Kendal, I guess that's what women do to a man. I glance over to Kendal and see she's crying just like Sophie."Right, now we have to go outside so they can clean this place ready for us to party and get drunk!"

Everyone cheers and raises their glasses to the happy couple and then make our way out of the marquee as staff rearrange tables and chairs. Outside, waiters are walking around offering drinks, I take one and spot Leo and Max over by the other side of the house all alone. I walk over as quietly as I can so they don't know I'm near, I want to hear what there whispering about. That's when I hear Leo. "Fucking hell man, why didn't you tell me she's bringing her son alone? What man fucking does that?"

"It wasn't my place to say anything. She looks like she's doing

OK."

"I wanna find him and show him a piece of my fucking mind."

I decide to step in. "Let me know when you have a name."

They both turn to me wide eyed, Leo steps on his cigarette and rubs his face with both hands. "Sorry man."

Max shakes his head and looks into the crowd, I do the same and see Kendal standing with Steph and Rex laughing. Max speaks but I'm still looking at Kendal. "Look at her Jax. How can someone do that to her?"

"Yeah well, I'm back now."

Kendal

"Look at those two, grinding on each other, you would think they were lesbians." I'm laughing as Jessica and I watch Tanya and Maisy dance. The reception has now started, I'm busy laughing at Tanya and Maisy when I feel someone tap on my shoulder. I quickly turn and it's Sam with James and Mark standing behind him.

"Tough day?"

I huff loudly and smile, I don't want people watching out for me tonight. I want us to all have fun. Tanya appears and grabs hold of my hand. "Come on Kendal, let's get drunk."

She drags me to where Maisy is standing at a tiny table that has drinks waiting. She hands me a shot of, I don't know what, but it burns my throat. Then a glass of vodka and lemonade, which I happily take from her. After dancing with them for a couple of songs I dismiss myself to go and ring Finley before I get too drunk. I walk through the big double doors into the house and into a quiet hallway. The phone only rings twice before Finley screams down the line. *"Hi mummy!"*

"Hey are you OK?"

"Yeah, I had pizza!"

"Are you being a good boy?"

"Yes!"

"Good."

"Cake mummy! Get the cake!"

I laugh and grimace at his panicked screeching down the phone. "Yes, I'll remember the cake Finley."

"Me and granddad watching Cars."

"Oh. I bet granddad's just loving that." I laugh, my dad hates Disney films.

"Granddad went night nights so I smacked his face to wake him up." I hear my mum laughing in the background and I can't help but laugh as well.

"Finley ,you shouldn't smack granddad."

"Sorry mummy but granddad was naughty. He has to watch it all."

"Okay, well I'm going now so night night and I'll see you tomorrow OK?"

"Okay, is the wedding boring?"

"Yeah really boring. Everybody is kissing and dancing."

"Errrrrrr Night mummy."

"Night Finley, love you."

"Love you mummy."

Just before I hang up I catch sight of Jax watching me smiling and then I hear a screaming from my phone."Jesus Fin stop shouting. What's the matter?"

"My cake mummy!"

"Yes I will remember the cake now go to bed."

"After Cars."

"Well be a good boy and you can have the cake."

"Good girl mummy."

"Night rock star."

He hangs up laughing, leaving me alone with Jax. Oh shit, I called Finley rock star in front of Jax.

"Rock star huh?"

"Erm.."Shit, I don't know what to say!

"Sure sounds like he wants some cake."He looks at me with a weird expression and I feel awkward."So, why rock star?"

My heart stutters, oh fuck."What?"

He laughs, probably at the stupid look on my face."You said, night rock star. I know you wasn't saying it to me."

"Yeah, he thinks he's a rock star. My dad takes him to Johnny's to play with them. My dad called him rock star one day and it stuck." Jonny is one of the guys my dad was in the band and I didn't exactly lie to Jax.

"Wow, your dad still plays?" I nod."Finley sounds like a cool kid."

We stand in an awkward silence. "Look Kendal, I don't want us to be awkward together. I really miss you, can we at least be friends?"

Friends with Jax? I miss him too and I hate it being like this between us. If he's moved back I'll be seeing him more. I know he will want to be in Finley's life when I tell him.

"Yeah, friends sound good."

"Can I have your number?"I don't know if that's a good idea,but I give it him anyway. I will need it for when I want him to come over to mine to tell him about Finley."It's good to talk to you Kendal. I really have missed you. No matter where I was, I was thinking of you. These past couple of days seeing you have been good."

"I'm proud of you Jax and I've missed you too." He nods slowly looking towards the floor."I'd better go and find everyone."

"Yeah OK. Have fun." I nod and try not to make it obvious I'm trying to walk away as fast as I can. I relax a little when I get outside and breathe in the fresh air. I join Tanya and Maisy for another shot and continue with their grinding and I can't stop laughing as Jessica shakes her head at me. Now I'm having fun.

After about an hour of dancing, I take a break and walk up to the table Jessica is sitting at with the guys. She sits herself on my knee. At first I think it's because she is really drunk but then she whispers in my ear. "Jax hasn't taken his eyes off you."

I don't answer, I'm dying to turn around and look at Jax. I can feel his eyes on me. Tanya interrupts us and pulls Jessica off my leg. "Come on you two! Let's dance, Sophie's joined us."

Chapter 27

After a long time on the dance floor with the girls, we're all in need of another drink so we all sway over to the bar, laughing all the way there. We chat with the guys at the bar and Rhys joins us and wraps his arms around Sophie. They look so happy.

"I'm so happy for you two."

"I'm glad you're here with us."

He pouts at me. Yeah, Rhys is drunk, along with most the people here. I poke his bottom lip that he's sticking out. "Me too, I missed you. You know you are the brother I always wanted right?"

And so the drunken soppiness begins. "Obviously, I've always thought of you as my little sister, you know that."

He grabs me in a tight drunken hug and I hear Sophie laughing. I know the drink is letting us speak our feelings but it is so true. I'm so happy for him and I love Sophie to bits. I'm so happy they found each other. Happy happy happy! I can't help but laugh when I hear the DJ announce the next song. "This is for Kendal and Max."

I hear the music start to *Nickelback's* song *Rock star* and I get a tap on my shoulder. I know who it is and when I turn to face Max, he's already singing along. I laugh and join in. He wraps his arms around my waist and lifts me off my feet. Max carries me to the main dancing area while we're singing to each other all the way there. He sets me down just as the chorus starts and we get into it like the good old days. Screaming in each other's faces and doing all the hand actions. Before I know it, the song has ended and on the last line he lifts me again, so our faces are level as we shout.

"Hey, hey I wanna be a rock star!"

We hug and before he lets me go he talks right into my ear. "Welcome back."

He brings tears to my eyes and I hear the cheering of our friends. I see Sophie, Jessica, Sam, Mark, James, Tanya, Maisy, Leo, Rhys and Jax all standing there with big smiles on their faces. Max leads me back to them near the bar and Sophie grabs me. "Kendal, that was awesome!"

I laugh a bit nervously from her compliment because having them all watching me shocked me a bit. I get a hug from Leo to. "Just like the good old days."

It's nice that everyone is getting along, the band and my guys laughing and joking together. I love the sight. I always wanted them all to get along. Mark has his arm wrapped around my shoulders and I chance a quick glance over at Jax and I'm shocked to see he doesn't look particularly happy.

Everyone cheers when *Swedish House Mafia - Don't You Worry Child* starts and we all dance together. I see Jax is now enjoying himself like the rest of us. It's amazing being back with everyone, like I've gone four years back in time. Only it's this time it's better because the band and the guys are actually having fun together.

We're on the dance floor together for a long time. Sophie joined in on our lesbian dance, and the guys obviously loved it. Even little Milly had a few dances with us before she went home. When the song, *I'm Sexy and I Know It* came on we all started dancing like crazy people. The guys are all over us and I can't stop laughing. Everything changes when the song ends and *Ne-yo's* song *Let Me Love You* comes on. I'm dancing with the girls and I feel strong arms hold onto my hips, even in my drunken state, my body reacts and I know its Jax. He looks down at me with an intense look in his eyes and I cannot help but melt inside. He leans down and talks directly into my ear so I can hear him over the music. That voice sends chills along my body. "Please dance with me."

His voice sounds pained, which is odd. I'm unable to answer because my body is going crazy, my throat is dry even though I've had more than enough to drink tonight. Instead of talking, I answer him by dancing against his hard body and I hear him groan. That low groan sends my body alight and I let my body melt into his. It feels so good to be so close to his warm, hard body. We're swaying together and I'm in my own little world, it's just me and Jax. My bottom is conveniently placed on his groin and I know for a fact he's enjoying this dance, it makes me extremely excited. My body is tingling all over, his big arms wrap around my waist and pull me closer so there's no space between us at all. He's totally in control, not letting me move away a little bit, not that I want to. He's always been an alpha male when it came to sex and I always loved it. Just thinking of it now has my underwear slightly damp with my arousal. Jax moves his head from my shoulder and kisses the back of my neck over and over. I'm covered in goose bumps and my body is full of need for him. A couple of slower songs start to play as it gets late into the night and the family's and young children have gone home, leaving just the adults.

I see Sophie and Rhys dancing, staring into each other's eyes to the left of us and I know Jessica will be grinding up on Sam somewhere too. Jax turns me around so I face him. I wrap my arms around his neck and he has his arms tightly around my waist, hands on the dip above my bottom. I totally lose myself to Jax.

Jax

"Dude, you gonna stare at Kendal all night?"

When I saw Kendal walk into the house, I followed her to speak to her alone. I overheard her conversation and I knew she had a great relationship with Finley. Now I can't seem to take my eyes from her.

Max and Leo walk up to us and hand us our drinks. "So, don't you think it's weird that her son's name is the same as your middle name?"

Well shit! How did I not realize that? "Fuck, I didn't think of that."

Rhys frowns at me and shakes his head. "Me either."

Kendal's had a child with another man and I feel kinda smug. I turn my attention back to the dance floor where Kendal is dancing with the girls. After our drinks are gone Max and Leo go back for more. It's good to see Kendal having a good time. I watch her sexy little body sway to the music. Sophie and Kendal are holding hands and singing the words to each other, I hear Rhys chuckle. "I love that those two get along so well."

"Yeah, they seem close." I see Max and Leo heading back in our direction and Max has a smug look on his face. What's he done now? "Why are you grinning like that?"

Max laughs and Leo shakes his head." I was buying the drinks and then I turn around and he's gone. He came back with that stupid look on his face."

Rhys groans and rubs his face with his free hand."Please tell me you haven't done anything stupid Max."

"Relax. I made a song request, that's all."About five minutes later, I hear the DJ and nearly choke on my beer, Max has a massive grin on his face."Step one in getting our girl back."

Chapter 28

I watch Max walk over to Kendal, *Nickelback's Rockstar* starts and I smile at the memories. I watch as he taps her on her shoulder and when she turns around she is laughing. She looks so fucking beautiful. Max lifts her up and carries her into the middle of the dance floor, both singing in each other's faces. Rhys motions with his head for me and Leo to follow him and we go and stand with Sophie who is standing with the rest of Kendal's friends, watching Max and Kendal.

After Max and Kendal's song we're all at the bar. I take sneaky looks across at Kendal and see she has another drink in her hand. Mark gets close and puts his arm around Kendal's bare shoulders. He laughs and talks while he's touching my woman and I'm suddenly more angry than jealous. I've let this creep have Kendal for four years. I bet he does everything he can to help Kendal out.

Later at night and we're all pretty drunk. I manage to get closer to Kendal as the songs continue and Max gives me a little wink. They want me to get with Kendal as much as I do. Watching her dance I can't fight it anymore, I have to get closer to her. I get right up to Kendal's back, the back of her neck bare because her hair is swept to the side. I reach my hands around her small waist and I feel her tense. Before she can tell me to go away, I lean down to the naked side of her neck and ask her to dance. She doesn't answer but instead dances against me so sweetly. Her sweet little arse keeps sweeping across my hard dick so I press against her harder. I rain kisses on her neck and lick her skin from her shoulder to under her ear. I can feel her shivering under me. I turn her around so I can see her face, I want to see those bright blue eyes. She wraps her shaky little arms around my neck, my hands are still around her waist but I want to grab on tight to her tight arse. She bites her lip, fuck it. I pull her closer so I can feel her tits squashed against me and reach down to grab that delicious little arse of hers. I've always loved her arse.

I can't believe my luck when the next song starts. Kendal gives me a shy smile because it's *Savage Garden-Truly, Madly, Deeply* and it's one of Kendal's old favorites. Until I met Kendal, I hadn't even heard it but since that night it's a song that holds a lot of good memories. I see Kendal blush and I know she remembers."Do you remember Kendal?"

Her blush deepens and she nods. The first time I heard this song was when I was at Kendal's one night, her parents were out. We had sex before then but this night was different. I knew I had fallen in love with Kendal. She had a playlist set up in her room and we started kissing as always, we never could keep our hands off each other. *Savage Garden's* song came on, and it changed the mood in the room. I looked down at my beautiful girl below me and I couldn't believe how lucky I was. I took control of the kiss and gave every inch of her body great attention during that song. Certain parts got more kisses than others. The song ended half way through my kissing so I put the song on repeat. I gave Kendal two loud orgasms with my kisses and tongue. By the end of her second orgasm, my dick was hurting so much I had to sink inside her heaven. Our sex was explosive and every time I became more and more addicted to her.

Now as the lyrics come through the speakers, I sing to her.

"I'll be your dream,
I'll be your wish,
I'll be your fantasy.
I'll be your hope,
I'll be your love,
Be everything that you need."

Kendal looks up at me with a shy smile on her face that makes me want to kiss her but I carry on.

"I'll love you more with every breath
Truly, Madly, Deeply do.
I will be strong

> *I will be faithful*
> *'cause I'm counting on*
> *A new beginning*
> *A reason for living*
> *A deeper meaning, yeah."*

I lean my cheek against hers and sing the chorus right into her ear. I know she's affected because she's still shivering.

> *"I want to stand with you on a mountain,*
> *I want to bathe with you in the sea,*
> *I want to lay like this forever,*
> *Until the sky falls down on me."*

I sing the next verse the same and when I look back at her face I can see tears in her eyes. I know what she's feeling because I can feel it too. My body wants her, it recognizes her. I lean my forehead onto hers, and look into her blue eyes and sing the rest.

> *"I'll be your dream,*
> *I'll be your wish,*
> *I'll be your fantasy.*
> *I'll be your hope,*
> *I'll be your love,*
> *Be everything that you need.*
> *I'll love you more with every breath,*
> *Truly, Madly, Deeply do"*

When the song finishes we stop dancing, but Kendal doesn't move her arms from around me. She didn't let her tears fall but I can still see them. Kendal licks her lips so I push my hard cock against her. I hear her give a little sigh, she wants this as much as I do and I slowly bring my face down closer to hers. I lightly brush my lips against hers, I let my tongue lick along her bottom lip. Kendal opens her mouth more, inviting me in. I don't wait any longer in taking her mouth. She kisses me back with just as much need, and I feel a groan escape me. Kendal moans a sexy purr against my mouth and then she's gone. I snap my eyes open to see Kendal standing in front of me with her hand over her mouth. A few tears fall down her cheeks but when I step closer she backs away from me.

"I can't Jax. This is too much. I can't, I'm sorry."

She turns around and walks as quickly as she can away from me. The girls following her. The guys all approach me and Rhys places a hand on my shoulder. "What happened?"

I shake my head, I don't actually know. I sang to her and we kissed but she kissed me back. Mark steps in front of me looking angry. "What did you say to her?"

"It's got fuck all to do with you."

"I think it has, seeing as I'll see her fall apart again." Sam steps between us and takes Mark away.

"Sooo, Kendal ran away after you kissed. You lost your touch?" I look at Leo who has a stupid grin on his face.

"Shut the fuck up." I look around, it's empty. I didn't realize we were only ones left here.

"Come on man." Rhys leads us towards the house and into his big dining room. He fetches us some beers, which I gladly start to drink.

"What's that?" Max points to the large packages on the other side of the table and goes to grab them. He peaks into the first bag and smiles. He lays it down on the table so we can all see it. It's a picture of the girls on a beach.

"These must be the pictures Sophie told me about. The girls had a photo shoot in Barcelona."

Rhys gets the rest of the pictures out of the other bags. In every picture, I just look at Kendal. She looks gorgeous in every picture. Max points to a picture of them all on a yacht, big sunglasses on, huge smiles. Fucking bikinis, I hope there were no men on that yacht. "I like this one."

Rhys frowns. "I hope a guy didn't take that."

Leo points to the picture of them all standing side by side, dressed up like they're going clubbing. Fucking hell, Kendal looks fuckable. I watch as Leo gets his phone out and snaps a close up of Tanya. Rhys shakes his head and carefully puts them back in the red bags.

Chapter 29

Kendal

I hear the girls shouting at me as I run to the safety of Sophie's house. It's good that our group are the only ones left here, this is less embarrassing with everyone gone. Once I'm inside the house, I run straight up the stairs and into the pink bedroom we all shared last night. Tanya is right behind me and grabs me into a tight hug, I can't help it when tears fall. All my girls surround me, either holding me or soothing me.

"I'm sorry for running."

Tanya releases me slightly but one of her arms is still protectively around me and Jessica is stroking my hair. "What happened?"

"I don't know. I panicked. I told you about that Savage Garden song right?" They all nod apart from Sophie. "That song, it holds a lot of strong feelings and memories for me. All of them with Jax, I even thought of it as our song. That night was one of the best nights of my life, oh god the things he did to me that night. Tonight, he sang every word to me. When we kissed it felt right. I know I love Jax but I can't do this. It's not right, he needs to know about Finley first."

All day I've looked at Jax and seen my little boy in him so much. Jax is a great guy and Finley is an amazing little boy and they both deserve to know each other. I can't keep them apart any longer.

Sophie decides to leave and make her wedding night official, leaving with a big smile on her face. I feel horrible I have caused drama on her big day but she assures me I haven't. We share the pink room again tonight. When Jessica returns from saying goodbye to Sam, she has two bottles of wine tucked in her arms and some plastic cups. We're all drinking our wine and gossiping, most of the drink gone when we hear a deep male laugh outside the door. I know that laugh, it's Max.

Tanya runs up to the door and listens for a few seconds and mouths Jax's name while pointing to the door. I jump up and so do Maisy and Jessica, we all press our ears against the door listening in. Yep, it clearly sounds like Max is laughing. I hear Jax who sounds really close to the door "Right, the girls are in there, my rooms there, so you two can choose from those."

"The girls are in the room behind you?"

"Yeah, that's the pink room. Why?"

"I was thinking of talking with Tanya. We need to sort some shit out." We all look at Tanya, who is now blushing."So something did happen between you two?"

We're all still looking at Tanya, who is now very red and biting on her bottom lip.

"Yes for fuck sake. We kept us a secret and I don't get why she doesn't want to talk to me. She's avoided me all day."

I raise an eyebrow at Tanya and she just shrugs her shoulders. I can hear Max laughing. "Aww, too bad."

"Whatever, I'm going to bed."

A door close by slams shut and we all creep away to sit on the bed again. Nobody speaks because we're all silent looking at Tanya. "Fucking hell guys, stop looking at me like that."

"You and Leo?"I whisper and Tanya rolls her eyes at me.

"It was ages ago. I really liked him and he was always flirting and one night after one of their gigs I finally gave in and it was fucking unbelievable. I mean wow, his dick is like."

Tanya's looking up the ceiling with a smile on her face. We all stay silent waiting for more details. "So it was amazing, the best and when we came out and back into the party some girls approached him and he's flirting with them right in front of me. He drops my hand like I'm a pile of shit and smiles at the girls like I'm not even there. I mean, I know we weren't together but we had just had sex for fucks sake! Show me some fucking respect. I didn't bother with him again after that. He tried to talk to me and hook up again but I said no. What he did hurt and I was not giving into him."

The bed starts bouncing, and I see that beside me, Jessica is on her knees bouncing and looking really excited. "Come on Tan! Details."

We all laugh at Jessica looking like an excited kid on Christmas. Maisy suddenly points at Tanya. "Wait! Is he the reason you wanted a dildo? You said after 'this guy' you could never get off with anyone else. Was that Leo?" Tanya's ducked her head. "He must be good."

"Ugh I don't want to think of Leo like that."

"Ignore her, now get with the details."

Chapter 30

Jax

I can hear the girls laughing from the next room. At least I know Kendal's okay because I was worrying I had really upset her. I'm trying my hardest to get some sleep, but I can't stop thinking about Kendal. I hear a thump, thump, thump noise, then some more laughing again.

"Go Kendal! Go Maisy! Go Kendal! Go Maisy!" What the hell are they doing in there?

After another half an hour it's gone quiet next door. I grab my phone and look through old pictures of me and Kendal. I haven't looked at them for almost two years, I couldn't delete them. I stop at one of my old favorites. It's the one I had printed out for her. I close down the photo and start to write a text message. She's probably fast asleep right now but I can't help myself.

ME: Hey its Jax. I can't sleep. I didn't mean to upset U. U looked amazing today
xxx

I hit send. I don't expect a reply from her. I just wanted her to know I'm sorry. I was surprised when my phone vibrated five minutes later.

KENDAL: Hey, I can't sleep either. I'm squashed between Jess + Tan. U didnt upset me. Jax, that was all me. I loved u singing 2 me again. I was just scared, I'm sorry I ran xxx

ME: Well I have my big bed all 2 myself. I'm glad I didn't upset u. I love all our old memories, I think about them a lot. R u staying 4 breakfast?xxx

After twenty minutes I drop my phone back onto the bedside table and try my best to get some sleep. Just as I'm finally drifting off I hear the loud sound of my phone vibrating.

KENDAL: I'm jealous of all that empty space in ur bed :p I love our memories 2, just being in ur arms again brought back feelings and they scared me. I didn't know what 2 do with them. I always think about u 2 Jax. We were good friends + I missed that. Yes I'm staying 4 some breakfast but I'm leaving at 12. U still on for that chat tomorrow? Seeing as I'm leaving in 6 hours I better try + get some sleep. Wish me luck with these bed hogging whores haha. I'll see u in the morning, if u can get up on time LOL xxx

ME: I look forward to making new memories Kendal. I've missed u allot. I want u back in my life. Yes I still want to come by tomorrow. Just let me no when + I will b there. Night Kendal xxx

Almost straight away I get her short reply.

KENDAL: Great, c u tomorrow. Night Jax xxx

Kendal

I hear a scream in my dream.

"Tan, wake up now!"

That was not my dream. I squint open my eyes enough to see Maisy standing at the side of the bed. She has her hands on her hips and she is scowling down at Tanya, who is lying on the bed laughing at Maisy. "I'm sorry Maisy. I was stretching."

"You kicked me on the floor!"

Tanya carries on laughing and that's when Jessica rolls over and slings her arm and one leg over my body. I take a look at her, she's still sleeping. "Erm Jess?"

Tanya stops laughing and turns to look at me. "Looks like Jess is missing her Sammy boy."

"She's just sleeping."

Jessica sighs in her sleep, scoots closer to me and rubs her hand along my stomach. "Mmmmmmm"

My eyes bug out wide while Maisy starts giggling. "Jess, get off me!"

Jessica's eyes pop open, I raise my eyebrows at her and nod to where her hand is still on my belly. She looks down but still does not move her hand or her leg. Instead, she grinds on my leg and smiles at me. "What do you say Kendal?" I shove her off a little bit harder than I was supposed to, so she rolls off the bed with a loud thud. "Hey!"

I scoot over so I can see her lying on the floor and I can't help but laugh. Very quickly Jessica reaches up and yanks me down on the floor too. I land on the floor beside her and then Tanya falls on top off me. What the hell? There are two double beds in here but four of us slept in the same bed"Ooohh, Kendal."

"You're all fucking weird! Get of me!"

Tanya gets pulled off me by Maisy. I know what they're doing, they're trying to make me forget about yesterday. After convincing them I'm okay, they eventually leave me alone. After we've packed our things and are ready it's 11:00. We go down to the dining room, I'm shocked to see everyone is here already. Sophie's hair is a bit on the wild side and she also has a highly satisfied grin on her face, the little tart. Tanya walks right up to her and kisses her cheek.

"By the looks of your hair and the smirk on Rhys face, you two definitely sealed the marriage. Did you use your new pole?"

I laughed as did everyone else while Sophie blushed. "Tanya! You're so embarrassing!"

I go and give her a hug and sit by her, still giggling. Sophie runs a hand through her mess of hair. "Oh Kendal it is a mess from all the hairspray and curls from yesterday. I forgot to take it out and I fell asleep."

I look at her in shock and behind me I hear Tanya gasp. "You left it in?"

"Why? Is that bad?"

Tanya pats Sophie's shoulder and shakes her head. "Honey, I need to go and get mine and Kendal's stuff because we need to rescue your hair."

"I can't believe you managed to sleep with all that in your hair."

"I was tired."

Sophie blushes again and bites her bottom lip. I look at Rhys who is sitting at the top of the table, with Jax at his side, both grinning at us. Tanya leaves the room while the guys are all laughing. I grab some toast that's in the middle of the table and eat some before Tanya returns. I can feel Jax looking at me and when I look up, he gives me such a cute and sexy smile. I hope I'm not blushing. He's looking very sexy this morning, which he probably always does. His hair is still a bit wet from his shower, jet black and sticking in every direction. He's wearing a plain white shirt that clings to his muscled chest and the sleeves look tight around his strong bulging arms. Oh god he looks edible, I want to eat him for breakfast rather than this toast.

"Good morning Kendal."

"Good morning Jax."

"Good morning Kendallllllll." Leo mocks Jax, which gets him a punch in his arm. Tanya walks in with a large handbag full of our hair products from yesterday. She sits back down next to me and hands me the necessary tools.

"Sorry Soph, but this might hurt a little."

"Just got for it, don't worry about going soft."

I hear Leo snort at her remark. I cringe while I rip through Sophie's hair, I hate that sound. I start on the second bottom section and it's just as bad. When it's all nice and smooth I gather it in a pony tail. I sit back down and see Jax is looking at me with a happy expression.

"What?"

He shakes his head and adorably looks a little embarrassed I caught him looking at me like that.

After some breakfast it's time for me to go. Sophie pouts and gives me a big hug. Rhys looks up from his food and asks if I'm leaving."Yeah, I'm meeting my mum back at mine."

Leo and Max are looking straight at me and don't look happy. Sophie jumps up, "Oh! I need to get little Finley some cake, wait one minute."

Sophie disappears into the kitchen, so I look back to Max and Leo. "What?"

Leo decides to answer me. "Why is your son at your parents?"

Why is he asking me that? He knows I'm a single parent, I return his glare. "Because I'm here with you guys." I don't understand why he's looking mad. "What is your problem?"

Max decides to step in seeing as Leo is not fucking talking. "We just don't like you being on your own. Leo's angry that this guy did that to you. We all are."

Oh shit! "That's my problem, not yours."

Jax scowls across at me. "Like fuck it isn't."Not now, just a few more hours Jax please!"Just tell me why he doesn't see his dad."

"No."

"Why not?" I shrug. I really can't answer that right now, not in front of everyone. He needs to wait until we're alone. "So his dad left you? Left you a single mother! Who is he? I'll kill that motherfucker."

"No, you won't. Just calm down."

"Why are you so calm?"

I stay silent. If I'm not careful, I will tell him here, which is not what I want. If people push me I blurt out the truth and Jax knows that. Leo decides to speak up. "Kendal, I'm sorry, but it makes me angry."

"You do not need to be. This is my problem, not yours."

Max stands up looking pissed. "It is now. You're like a sister to me."

Leo follows and also stands banging his fist on the table, making me flinch. "We get the job of making sure that bastard is there for you. Now who is he?"

I'm starting to sweat. Shut up, shut up, shut up! I'm shaking so much. Thankfully Tanya helps me. "Guys, sit down and shut up. Look what you are doing to her. Leave her alone."

Sophie returns with a little bag."Right, I've got the little man some cake and I took some sweets from Rhys' secret stash."

I stand and take it from her. I need to get out of here before everything spills out my mouth. Jax deserves to be told in private and I want to give him that. The girls stand up with me, and we all say our goodbyes. I smile at the guys, who are still scowling. I need to go.

Chapter 31

Jax

The guys all look to me when the girls leave and Sophie walks them to their cars. I try and ignore Rhys. "Was there any need for that?"

"I didn't mean to, it just pisses me off. How can someone do that to her?"

"A fucking prick is who."

"I say we find out and pay him a little visit."

I look around at my friends at the table and try to calm my anger. "How can someone do that to a woman? How can you look at Kendal and walk away from her while she's pregnant with your baby? If that was me, I would never walk away."

The fact that someone got my Kendal pregnant and fucking left her all alone gets me so fucking angry! I want to go tell this low life to face up to his responsibilities. I don't know why Kendal didn't look angry herself, she just looked sad. I know if I keep pushing Kendal I will get the truth. She's like a time bomb when she's hiding something, push her enough and she explodes.

I walk out the dining room with the guys following me. The girls are still in the main entrance, saying their goodbyes to Sophie. I take a step toward Kendal and everyone goes quiet. "Can I still come today?"

"I'll text you, okay?"

She doesn't sound very happy." I'm sorry I upset you in there. Why are you not angry about it?"

"I'm more upset than anything Jax."

"Then tell me who he is and I will see to it."

"Don't be silly."

I take her hand in mine."Let me help you, I can take care of you both."

"I don't need your help Jax! I've looked after Finley perfectly fine on my own!"

"I'm not saying that."

The guys stand by close, the tears in her eyes hurt me. Rhys decides to step in."Kendal, we just want to help you by being here for you."

She calms a little, until Leo steps in."Tell me where he lives and I will be over there right away."

"Leo! Leave it please!"

Why doesn't she want to tell us who Finley's dad is?"Why is it such a secret?"

Jessica places a hand on Kendal's shoulders."Why don't you and Jax go and talk outside."

But she shakes Jessica off and shakes her head."No."

"What aren't you telling me?"

"I've got to go."

I hold onto her wrist and stop her from walking away. I can feel her breaking and she's going to crack soon. Just a little bit more."Kendal, please tell me."

"Just leave it alone"

Her broken voice hurts me, but I carry on."Why is it a big secret?"

"Please, get off me Jax."

"Tell me!"

Max comes next to me and I know he's going to help Kendal get away but she's nearly there.

"Jax, let me go."

She tries to pull away but she has no success. The girls are surrounding her and look like they could cry any minute.

"Tell me who it is."She ignores me and keeps pulling away. The girls try, but Leo and Max stop them from coming any closer. "Who is the selfish bastard? He must be bad if you don't want him to know."

She looks shocked and shakes her head."No! He's not like that."

"Why are you protecting him?"

"You've got it all wrong. Just let me go!"

Maisy shouts from behind Max."Jax, just let her go and calm down please."She sounds like she's crying now.

"Kendal, just tell me who it is and you can go"

"Not yet. Later, OK?"

"Why?"

"Please Jax, let me tell you later."

Why does she want to tell me later? No, she won't tell me. This is a trick."Kendal!"

"No!"She falls to the floor and starts to cry. I've let go of her wrist so she turns onto her knees and goes to run away. I get on the floor and catch her around the waist. I turn her around to face me, her face is all wet."No Jax, please don't."

"Tell me Kendal."

"No."She's sobbing now. I look up and everyone is frozen in place looking down at us. What a fucking sight. The guys look as shit as I feel and the girls are all crying. All this happening the day after Rhys and Sophie's wedding.

"Tell me, I can help you!"She doesn't answer. She just looks at me and cries."Kendal, please just tell me."

"I can't"She whispers.

"Kendal! I won't let you go until you tell me,"

"It's you, Jax!"

"What?"

She turns to glare at me and I let her go. She shuffles away from me."IT'S YOU! ARE YOU HAPPY NOW? YOU! YOU ARE FINLEYS DAD!"

I sit back and just stare at her. Did she really just say that? Is it true?"What, you don't believe me? You've gone all quiet on me?"

I swallow hard and just continue to stare. How can she lie like this? Surely she's not telling the truth. How can she do that to me? Kendal stands up and grabs her bag, the girls stand close by her.

"I was going to tell you today when you came around. I was going to let you finally meet him. I can't believe you did this to me."

She quickly turns around and leaves but I see her tears. Maisy follows her outside leaving Jessica, Tanya, and Sophie standing there glaring at me with their arms folded. Jessica points at me. "I can't believe you did that to her! How dare you!"

Tanya stomps over and slaps me hard. "You fucking forced that out of her, you bastard!" Tanya starts to cry. "She torn herself up every day for not telling you. How could you?"

She cries harder and Leo comes over but she stops him. "Don't you fucking dare! You held me back from helping her, get away from me!"

She shoves him out the way and goes to hug Sophie and walk out, leaving Sophie standing on her own glaring at me. "I know she's no angel, but that was wrong Jax."

Rhys helps me up and stops his wife from talking. "He just heard he has a son Soph, cut him some slack.

Sophie leaves in a huff.

"I'm sorry this happened. I brought all my drama to your wedding."

"No you didn't. It's fine."

He walks after Sophie, leaving me with Max and Leo.

"I can't believe Kendal would do that."

Leo heavily sighs. "You've not heard Kendal's side yet."

I scoff. "So you think keeping my son away from me is a good idea?" They don't answer, so I rub my face and groan loudly.

"How can she do this to me? I fucking loved her! That's my son, how can she not tell me I'm a dad. I've wasted three years away from him, from Kendal, sleeping with sluts when I could have been with them!"

Max shakes his head and says, "Maybe that's why she did it."

"What?"

"Maybe she didn't tell you because of the girls? She did say that yesterday she felt like she was keeping you back."

"So you're telling me she raised my son alone so I could sleep around?"

I love Kendal and she does this to me. I can't do this right now. I need to get out of here. I thought I was angry before, but now I'm fucking fuming! How could she keep my son away from me? I don't know if I'm angrier at Kendal for keeping Finley away from me or the fact I have missed so much. I could have been here for them, been a dad to Finley and been with Kendal. I don't know what I should do, but I do know that I still want Kendal and I will be a part of my son's life.

If you liked Rockstar Daddy and want to find out what happens next with Jax, Kendal and Finley.
Follow me on Twitter at https://twitter.com/ktfisher_author
Like me on Facebook at
https://www.facebook.com/#!/pages/KTFisher-Author/490003474414733?fref=ts
to hear updates on my books or to get in touch.

Printed in Great Britain
by Amazon.co.uk, Ltd.,
Marston Gate.